PRAISE

MW00424756

*"A twisted and cinematic new series."*

LUKE JEROD KUMMER, AUTHOR OF *TAKERS
MAD* AND *THE BLUE PERIOD*

*"An atmospheric riveting thriller you won't be
able to put down or easily forget. One of Goldberg's best."*

TERRENCE MCCAULEY, AWARD-WINNING
AUTHOR OF *THE WANDERING MAN* AND *THE
MOSCOW PROTOCOL*

# DESIRE'S END

## THE DESIRE CARD BOOK FIVE

# LEE MATTHEW GOLDBERG

ROUGH
EDGES
PRESS

**Desire's End**
Paperback Edition
Copyright © 2022 Lee Matthew Goldberg

Rough Edges Press
An Imprint of Wolfpack Publishing
5130 S. Fort Apache Rd. 215-380
Las Vegas, NV 89148

roughedgespress.com

Paperback ISBN 978-1-68549-152-9
eBook ISBN 978-1-68549-151-2
LCCN 2022944093

# DESIRE'S END

"Not necessity, not desire—no, the love of power is the demon of men. Let them have everything—health, food, a place to live, entertainment—they are and remain unhappy and low-spirited: for the demon waits and waits and will be satisfied."

**—— Friedrich Nietzsche**

A THREE-DAY BOAT RIDE FROM YURIMAGUAS TO Iquitos after a month-long one from the Port of Manzanillo where William Clark fled. Some strained business occurring with a cartel that he was choosing to cleanse from his mind. The Amazon called to him, the lung of the planet, rather ironic since his lungs were tar black and in danger of inhaling their last breaths. Too many Mayan Sicars cigars, a perk from when he ran the Desire Card under his alias Clark Gable. Now he's an old, old man with a knot the size of a grapefruit on his back, trembling fingers, and a cough that makes sleeping difficult. Well, that and a target for his head served on a platter with an apple in his mouth.

He was used to being in a tight squeeze. The first time when the feds closed in on him and he escaped across the border to Mexico, he laid low for a while but then got bored. Isn't that what the concept of desire is after all—a way to alleviate the boredom? At least once that final breath will occur, he'd never be accused of living a boring existence. He always said with a chuckle that when he goes, he'll be erupting in flames.

He had a contact in Mexico who ran a shipping cargo. A month on the waters with the smell of chicken shit and his associate The Doctor as a roommate in tense quarters. The Doctor also pushing eighty with a rattling cough that sounded like a pissed off ghost. Both of their bellies bloated from a diet solely of chicken and eggs. He can still taste the phantom burps.

Now pigs have taken the place of The Doctor on this new smaller vessel via the Huallaga and the Marañón Rivers. Once in Iquitos, he hid his ugly mug and wound through the neighborhood of Belen with floating houses on the river and overpaid for a bus to take him into the Amazon. After a five-hour journey where he puked up his lunch of turtles from the market because of the bumpy roads, he was let off in the middle of what seemed like nowhere. He told the guide to forget he ever saw him and paid handsomely before slinging his pack over his shoulder and hiking the rest of the trek.

The jungle hooted and swayed around him. A growl in the distance. A spider crawling over his foot. A monkey clinging to a tree. The sun a hot guide pulling him along trails that few ever wound down. When the sun set, the sky turned the kind of purple of other worlds before it sparkled and tag-teamed the night. He had a tiny lantern that allowed him to only see his feet in front of him, but he knew the way because he'd been called and the map existed in his heart.

The sky showed a grab bag of stars. Tiny pinpricks that soon helped light the way. He was hungry and dehydrated but with death so close, he did not fear anything. Not what existed at the end of this journey. He had never feared anything in his long life and that was why he was so successful.

This calling from deep within the jungle had reached out before. Many times over the past two to three decades in fact. But it pinched him with greater frequency once he settled in Mexico. Maybe because he was closer in location. Maybe because he was closer to death. All of those dying could hear a hum that others couldn't—the shifting from one world to the next.

And what would that world be? If he believed in heaven or hell—which he didn't—but if he did, he was sure to wind up below. Four decades at the Card and the body count he left behind—even along this final journey—too high in number to guess. There was a small circle for those like him if hell existed. A long time ago he understood there was nothing he could do to keep him from that evil caucus.

But the very notion of evil is something he's wrestled with since he began this dark tenure. A war erupts and soldiers fight and kill, neither believing they are the evil ones. It is in the eye of the beholder, he has decided. And who made the rules? Who decided laws? He did, that's what he will tell you. And the rules he decided on had one main tenet—not that he believes in God, but his rule is that he is a God of his own path. Therefore, whatever he decides is how it shall be. And anyone who falls in the crosshairs, simply unlucky.

Tell that to his daughter Helene whose own daughter went missing. Tell that to his granddaughter Gracie who he kidnapped as collateral. Tell that to his son-in-law Harrison who was desperate enough to use him to get a liver off the black market. Or JD Storm, who once worked for him as his very best operative, foolishly choosing to try and retire. Or his son Chip who wound up dead. Or Cagney, or Stewart, or Bogart, or Errol Flynn, or any of the other operatives or station agents that he rehabilitated with brand-new masks of legends to hide their scars only to wind up six feet under. Or his wife Vivienne or Audrey Hepburn or beautiful Marilyn Monroe who were crazy enough to love him. And he loved each of them, in their own way, even though to love him meant flirting with possible death. Tell that to The Doctor most recently who met his fate with a bullet and was plunged into the icy cruel waters. This is William Clark's design, a path of broken glass, bloody feet and a smile like a scar. A path filled with billions of dollars and desires. A path of decomposing bodies.

———

William Clark walks through the jungle shaking from lack of food for what seems like an eternity. If he died along the way and this was his afterlife, he wouldn't be surprised. An endless trail getting feasted on by mosquitos, the cold seeping into his bones now that the sun has gone. One of his feet gone to rot and blistering. A limp becoming more pronounced. Just when a trail seems to open up and he thinks he has arrived at his destination, he's met with emptiness and forced to hack through thickets of branches in the hopes that he will reach his destiny soon.

Even though he has been called by this force, this energy, or whatever it is, he has no clue what he is in store for. A bullet to his head, the final plan to take him out. No. There is no way he will go that easily. Even if this means his death, he'll go out swinging with fire and fury.

There's an unhinged feeling knowing no one will find his body here. He will disappear into the ether like he's done before, a mystery never solved. Just like the devil. More powerful as an enigma to fear than a reality. And who remaining would even miss him? Most people spend their lives focusing on creating close relationships, he will be buried with no one hovering over the body to mourn his passing. His daughter wants nothing to do with him anymore. His wife the same now that his alias has been revealed. His granddaughter would spit on his ashes. Anyone he's loved met their maker long before, with the exception of Marilyn if she's even still alive. She took off in the night forty years ago with his possible child in her belly, never to be heard from again. Something he is trying to emulate.

A roar erupts echoing in the shaken trees. Likely a jaguar, for even though he's not far into the Amazon, jaguars run the land. That would be a fitting end, he thinks. Man versus beast as he'd succumb to death in its jaws. But like anything else, he'd put up a damn good fight. He was a Depression baby after all, his generation born swinging.

Out of the corner of his eye, a jaguar appears, its beautiful black coat shining in the moonlight. It locks its yellowed-eye gaze, pupils like opals. It bares its teeth, flanked with blood. If he were it, he'd devour him whole, but the jaguar simply observes. There's a similarity between the two. Both titans of their own jungles. Both with blood-stained teeth after a lifetime of kills. The jaguar smells this kindship, prowls around and tucks its head under his arm. It purrs beneath his hands for it understands his soul. The jaguar has destroyed anything in its way, it has fed on bones for survival. He almost weeps since no other creature has ever understood him so well. But he does not shed a tear, for William Clark doesn't cry. He is incapable.

The jaguar licks his palm, transfers its powerful energy. Silently says that no matter what happens on this twisted journey, he has an ally. And then it takes off, blending into the night, making him question if it ever was here or whether he's hallucinating.

And then, in the quiet distance, a tiny hut lit by a fire. Had the jaguar brought him here? He blinks, unsure if it's another hallucination. His water source bone dry, only memories of hydration left to carry him forward. Each step a lifetime, his body weighing a thousand tons. He shuffles closer to the hut only for it to appear even further away. There are no stars existing above its location, as if it doesn't truly exist on this plane.

The wind picks up, the trees growing angry. They beat against one another. The earth swirls dust beneath his soles. The wind picks up his step, pushes him forward until he is carried to the hut's wonky door.

From the outside, the hut appears no different than any basic shelter made of fallen branches and crinkled leaves. The door a dark mouth occasionally licked by the circle of flames. He peers inside and can see nothing but never-ending darkness. A buzz in his ear whispers not to enter, but it is short lived, since he is already propelled forward, thrust inside this gaping maw as his lantern goes out.

He is only left with his thoughts.

Until a new flame ignites.

So quickly he pats himself as if he's caught fire too.

It's just a blue flame dancing at the far end of the hut.

Revealing an old, old woman with long gray hair covering her face.

"Welcome," she says, although it doesn't sound like he is welcome at all.

## 2

WILLIAM CLARK STUDIES THIS OLD WOMAN, LIKELY around the same age as him, even though she appears more battered by life if that is possible. She wears a shawl that her coat hanger shoulders barely hold up. Two stick arms slither from out of the shawl, the veins purpling, the bones so close to the skin as if they are about to burst through. Her gray hair is parted in two, each long loom covering half her face with a wrinkled mouth poking out. The lips turned as if she tasted a sour lemon.

The hut's door shuts as he clutches his heart, a pinch radiating through his left arm. Every scare taking him that much closer to a heart attack that will end it all. Collapsed on this dirt ground as the old woman observes his passing. He pictures her cooking his newly dead body over a flame, plucking off his limbs, and gnawing with her sour mouth and loose teeth.

From behind him, he can feel the shadows move and a person standing in front of the door. This person has muscles, seeming to be the old woman's bodyguard.

The bodyguard crosses his thick arms, a roadblock to an escape. Something tells him he will never leave this hut again.

"Welcome," the old woman says again, her voice quivering. He thinks of one of the cruelties of life, the loss of one's original voice. His own used to be booming, commanding, now it's meek and full of phlegm. No one would ever take him seriously anymore. All they see when they look at him is death's embrace.

"I am unsure what brought me here," he says, realizing he's thirsty. Each word feels like a knife.

As if she knows, she nods to the muscle in the back who brings him a wooden cup filled with some kind of liquid. It's way too viscous to be water. The smell a mixture of sulfur and coins.

"Yes, drink," she says, miming how it should be done. "You need to rejuvenate."

He's too exhausted to probe, so he tips his head back and chugs. The oily cocktail pours down his throat, thick like tar. When it settles in his belly, his stomach makes growling sounds like it's fighting with this new substance for dominance over what will control his body.

At first, nothing. The drink hasn't quite settled but there is no difference from when he first sipped.

"What was it?" he asks.

"Illumination," the old woman says. Delight rings in her voice. "To see you. Truly. Has anyone ever truly seen you before?"

His hands go up to his face, usually where a Clark Gable mask resides. But ever since the surgery and fleeing the States years ago, he no longer requires that visage. Under the knife, they took Jay Howell's old face and left him average. Even without the mask, he had a presidential countenance. The moths drawn to his wild flame. He was a captain of industry, feared and idolized, worshipped by his family. Now he was nondescript, ordinary, no one ever bothering to look twice. It helped him in Mexico where he was seen as an old *gringo*. For the first few years, he anticipated the feds tracking him down, but they never showed. His case in the States moved to cold. Wars and plagues took over the news cycles. He was relegated to a footnote, an era in America when wealthy white men got away with their deceit. He was spoken about only by the conspirators, the tin hats with Coke-bottle glasses who lived in bunkers and thought of him as their next revolution. Elvis would be dead now anyway, even if he had lived, and he became the new Elvis for a moment. Everyone spotting Gable, screaming for their rewards until his name was met with a shrug.

"No one has ever really seen me before," he replies, as if tiny hands are tinkering with his vocal chords and forcing this response.

The thought, chilly. But also, a relief to admit. He had spent a lifetime without ever letting anyone get too close. For what lived inside of him was rotting.

"Why?" she asked, cocking her head to the side.

He pictures this rotting heart of his dripping blood on a stake as the flies swirl and she plucks it to devour with her sour mouth.

"I am human, but..."

He rubs his tired jaw as he tries to form what he means to say.

"I have never...felt human, at least for as long as I can remember. Maybe all sociopaths feel that way."

"You lack remorse?"

"I have no remorse, never had."

"What about with your son?" she asks, cocking her head to the other side.

The flames cooking the hut spit and crackle. The movement of the shadows loom closer. They swirl into his boy Chip before morphing to Chip as a man and then a cadaver.

A stabbing sensation plagues his heart. "How did you know?"

She lets out a chuckle that stabs him even harder. "You told me."

"When?"

"You always have."

"I don't...understand."

"I see," the old woman snaps, culling the flames that lick her hidden face. "I've seen you. Always. It is my capabilities."

"Like a shaman, you are a shaman."

"Yes, I am a studier. I observe."

"Like a God?"

"I thought you don't believe in God."

"I don't. Wait, how did you know that?"

"You told me."

"When?"

"You always have. God has been a fictional creation to you. Nothing more. It's how you've allowed yourself to..."

"To what?"

The shadows above appear to be fighting with one another.

"Absolve your sins. You simply absolve them to yourself. No mess, no fuss."

"We are naïve to think we are judged."

"Says the soul who has the most to be judged."

He lets out a cough that's ringed with blood. In his fist, a flash of death. A black spot in the center of his palm. His throat scratchy.

"Is the drink...?"

"Melding with your body?" She gives a firm nod. "Yes. It is taking control."

The hut pivots, rights itself, and then pivots again as if he's on a spiraling plane. He finds his balance.

"Who are you?" he asks, a string of drool dribbling from his lips.

The old woman shakes a finger. "I am not on trial here. I am just a conduit."

He laughs, a solitary bark. "So that's what this is, a trial?"

Her sour mouth manages to smile. "Of sorts."

"You tabulated all my sins and this is the precipice? You decide whether I go...up?" He raises his bushy eyebrows. "Or down?"

"No. This is not about you entirely."

"Then who is it about?"

"All that your tentacles have affected."

He chews on her phrase, tries to decipher its meaning.

She culls the fire until a thin layer of smoke permeates through the hut. "Your actions have had consequences to those you have pulled into your world. That is what you are you here to witness."

Inhaling a gust of smoke, she begins to shake like an epileptic. Her hands raise to the sky. Lightning storms break out, the rain a steady drumbeat. She faces him and spits the gust of smoke so it settles on his eyelashes, curls into his nostrils. The shadows on the wall become clearer, no longer darkened but morphing into high definition.

"You have called me for years," he says, resigned to whatever punishment will occur.

"You have only listened now."

"Why?" The shadows start to form into the shape of a girl.

"Because you are ready," the old woman says.

She nods at the muscled bodyguard in the back who comes behind him and gently lays him down on the hard ground. His head gets propped up by his backpack. He is given a blanket because the rainstorms have made it cool. The shadow swirls overhead as the old woman stamps her feet. She has gnarled toes that twist over one another, the nails long and curling like a French horn. He used to play one as a child, leaning out the window of his bedroom and sending the notes into the night. Was that the last time he knew true happiness?

"Can you see?" the old woman asks now. Spittle has collected on the edges of her lips, her tongue violent and red. She points to the top of the hut where an image of the girl materializes. It is his granddaughter Gracie who he kidnapped when she was only ten to use as collateral if necessary. But Gracie had been a surprise. She fought him at first, a petulant child, but soon became an asset. When the Card mutated into more of a sex trafficking ring, Gracie's job was to soothe the girls. Down in the underground lair, she would visit nightly, convince the girls that this would better their lives. By the age of thirteen she was luring naïve strays into vans who would never see their families again. By fourteen, she was recruiting—basically his station agent, which took operatives years to ascend to back in the old days of the Card. This was a new Card and for years he was convinced she had found her purpose. She was meant to be kidnapped by him and separated from her parents so she could realize her true potential. So it shocked him when she turned, their entire time in Mexico a performance worthy of an award.

Yet, he's fond of her—more than he could say about most of the human race. Wherever she wound up, he wishes her well. No ill will because that is reserved for those who truly tried to bring him down. Gracie saw an opportunity and took it. He is cut the same, so how could he blame her? She has ruthless DNA, and even if she finds her way back to America with her family, the Card is a part of her now. She is no longer a normal fourteen-year-old girl. That is solely because of his tentacles.

"So this is to be my Ebenezer Scrooge moment?" he asks.

The old woman shakes her head. "You won't be joking for long once the liquid truly kicks in."

In his veins, he receives a jolt. His eyes peel back until he's unable to close them. Gracie's in motion as if he's watching a film unspool. A window into what happened when she betrayed him and where she headed. He glimpses her running barefoot through the streets. Swiveling her head around to see if he or one of his operatives is following. A truck backfires that she thinks is a gunshot so she collapses to the ground. But she gets herself back up, she keeps on moving, uncaring about her sliced-up feet and the trail of blood she leaves in her wake.

## 3

GRACIE WOUND UP BEING PASSED ALONG FROM ONE kidnapper to the next, although she never imagined the last abductor to be her grandfather, Papa Jay. She'd always admired her grandfather. He never gave affection easily, only if it was earned. When he walked into a restaurant or a charity gala, he commanded respect. Let's be honest, her family were not the best role models. Her father weak and distant, gluttonous and often bored. Her mother forever harping on her father's faults. Her grandmother a snob. So out of all of them she'd choose Papa Jay and got a thrill whenever he'd pay attention.

They had a similar personality, even at her tender age of nine. Gracie was focused and diligent, quiet and elegant. Papa Jay poured his energy into his business with a dedicated obsession (even though she didn't quite know what he did), and she gave the same enthusiasm to ballet. The plan was to be a world-renowned dancer, at least before the kidnapping occurred.

The question: why did he take her? Papa Jay had

been exposed as a criminal mastermind and needed something to barter, in case it came to that. If the authorities descended, he could always give back his sweet granddaughter as a show of good-nature. So at first, he kept her hidden in a room with a tiny barred window that overlooked a weedy lawn. She knew she was in Mexico because she overheard the bodyguards talking and had been taking Spanish (and French mind you) since first grade at her fancy private school. Where in Mexico, she had no idea. Even if she did, it was unlikely to help her situation. If she missed her family, it was just too bad. This was her home, and her future. She better get used to it.

The bodyguards fed her three times a day and she had an attached bathroom, which was better than her last abduction situation. And she wasn't chained anymore. She could dance in her little room, going through her entire Swan Lake performance from a year ago over and over again in a desperate attempt to stay sane. She wouldn't speak to Papa Jay when he'd deign her with his presence, even though he was always kind and contrite. He'd sit on the edge of her thin mattress and explain how he "had to take her." Sometimes he would shake his fist. "You were in too much danger," he'd add, as tiny spittle formed at the corners of his lips.

One day, he showed up with a plate of enchiladas and extra cheese, since she loved that and he actually apologized.

"I'm sorry," he said, swallowing the words as if they were made of nails. "And I don't apologize often, so consider yourself lucky. It is an untenable situation, but I say we make the best of it. You don't have to stay in this room."

One eye of hers crept to the side, observing but untrusting.

"I am in the process of starting a small-scale business here."

"In Mexico?" she chirped. It was the most she said to him since she arrived. His eyebrows raised.

"How did you know?"

"I speak some Spanish. Your bodyguards were talking."

She pointed a thin finger toward the door where the two bodyguards were, in fact, having a raucous conversation in Spanish.

"Smart girl. So..." He held out his hand as if he was inviting her to high tea. "Shall we? Will you be a good girl?"

She gave him a lopsided grin. Having not decided yet how she'd behave, she figured it was better to go along than to remain trapped. She'd pictured what the house looked like outside of the room, but it was really a dump. Wood paneling. Chipped paint. Chickens clucking by the windows. A lone television that seemed far older than her. Two men in masks of old-time movie stars watching the news on a ratty sofa. They turned to her in unison.

"Brando. Astaire," Papa Jay said. "Meet my granddaughter. Gracie."

They gave a curious wave.

On the news, bodies hung from streetlights due to a cartel's rampage. She found their swaying calming and sat down next to the men in masks.

"You are free to roam this house," Papa Jay said.

A chicken clucked.

"And outside?" she asked.

"If you behave."

She observed her fingernails. The nail polish she had used weeks ago had chipped with bits still clinging.

"I want to dance."

Brando and Astaire chuckled before Papa Jay gave them a look that shut them up good.

"Ballet, right?" he asked.

He had never been to any of her performances. She knew her grandfather didn't have time for what he deemed trivial. It surprised her he even remembered.

"Maybe we can work something out."

A fire burned in her belly. The excitement palpable in her grinding teeth. She had gotten in the habit of plucking out her hairs and her fingers traveled to a tiny bald spot that sprouted.

"Thank you," she said. Although it would be weeks until she could dance with an actual teacher in a studio. What Papa Jay wanted came first... For to be in her grandfather's good graces meant doing favors.

The initial 'errands' took her down to the basement where teenage girls lazed in cages. She walked down a hallway ringed by the girls on both ends, their eyes glassy and off in another world, a better one than their current location. They were unwashed and smelled ripe. They moaned in the night and initially made her shiver. They seemed unable to use their limbs or even move. The most energetic of the bunch slipped her fingers through the cage reaching out for a connection.

Gracie craned her head to Papa Jay, her eyes asking a myriad of questions.

"They have a job to do," he said. "They are getting ready. Keep them company. Occupy their time."

He left with a lone light swinging from the ceiling.

It was dark but a sea of eyes watched her with fascination. They wondered why she was free while they stayed imprisoned. She began to dance.

It was difficult without her ballet shoes to hit the marks, but she tried to give these girls as strong a performance as she could. For an hour she kept them enraptured. When she ended, she could hear a few cry. They began speaking to her, but she didn't want to hear any of it. She retreated up the stairs.

That was how her days were filled. She had meals outside of her room, usually with Brando and Astaire, two sad men that ate the same daily porridge. Once it turned nighttime, she'd descend to the basement and dance until she could barely keep her head up. After some time, she'd notice a few girls went missing, never to return. They were doing their job, she figured. It was good for them to leave.

Each night they all would light up when she entered. The ones who hadn't left yet had grown thin, their ribs on display. Sometimes she'd hear them whispering to each other in Spanish. She learned they were mostly local girls, plucked off the streets. They had been homeless, or without families who'd look for them. They spoke of two men in masks who whisked them into a van and sped off. One drove while the other stuck them with a needle. They went to sleep and awoke in this basement.

Gracie had her first birthday since she'd been taken. Turning ten, she felt old, like she'd seen too much in this short life for her small body to compute. That night, she told the girls about her birthday and they murmured congratulations. In Spanish she asked them how old they all were, surprised to learn that while most were sixteen, seventeen, a few of them were thirteen, even twelve. One girl said she was eleven. She had big doe eyes and a dot of a mouth. She was taller than Gracie, stooped in her cage, her arms like broomsticks. She had such long hair Gracie thought of Rapunzel. After Gracie would dance for the others, they would go to sleep, but this girl never did. She spoke English, using the show *Friends* to teach herself before she ran away from home. When Gracie asked why, she responded that her father was a bad man who did bad things. Gracie thought of her own father and understood. She'd never actually run away but had considered what it'd be like. Now that she knew, she was surprised that she didn't long to go home. She didn't want to be here, or anywhere really. She wanted a different life and to start again.

"What will they do with me?" the doe eyed girl asked.

Gracie was tracing a circle into the ground with her toe. She'd imagined what became of these girls. What types of jobs they were tasked to do. It couldn't be great if they needed to be locked up to agree.

An older girl across the room overheard and started yelling. It was in Spanish and very fast, so Gracie had a hard time understanding everything, but she did pick up that the older girl was talking about sex and being a slave. The more she said, the more the doe-eyed girl shivered.

At ten, Gracie knew very little about sex. She wasn't naïve to its existence. Her school had health classes and she'd seen it on TV. Back home, a girl in her class named Vita had let a boy touch her down there. All the other girls were rapt. Gracie thought it a waste of time. Would sex make her a better ballet dancer? If it wouldn't, then what was the point? She felt sorry for these girls that it would occupy so much of their time.

"What if I don't wanna?" the doe-eyed girl asked.

"Don't want to what?" Gracie asked.

"Sleep with..." She lowered her voice to a hiss. "Men."

Now the puzzle came together. These girls were taken and then pawned off on men who in turn paid Papa Jay. She didn't answer the girl and left the basement. Upstairs, Papa Jay smoked a cigar and had a "snort" of alcohol, as he would say. She slinked up behind him.

"I know what you do."

He swiveled around. "Come again?"

She was aware she breathed very heavily. "The girls. I know what you do with them."

"Oh, do you?"

"I can help."

He squinted his eyes, likely not expecting that response. He ran his finger along the edge of his glass and made it sing.

"How can you help?"

"I've been dancing for them downstairs, giving them something to take their minds off of... I could do more than that."

He nodded for her to continue.

"They are afraid. I can make sure they aren't. Make them believe they are here for other reasons."

Papa Jay ashed his cigar, then inhaled.

"I suppose you want something in return?"

She nodded carefully. "I want to dance."

"You dance for the girls."

"Outside. Of this house. Let me go outside."

He shook his head. "Too dangerous."

"For who?"

"There are many people who want me taken down. You could be a means to that."

"What if..." She nibbled on her lip. "What if there was a ballet studio? With a private teacher. A bodyguard could supervise. And I'm driven there and then brought right back. You could pay off the teacher so they won't say anything."

"You've thought about this?"

"The girls. They know what you are doing to them. It is all they talk about downstairs. They are frightened. That can't be good. But I can make up something else they are used for. What if we told them...they will be working for very rich families, doing errands? That some bad people are after them but they are being kept safe here."

The cherry of Papa Jay's cigar glowed orange as he inhaled again.

"Keep talking."

"They are not here for long, right? Just till you find the...men for them. You want it to be as quiet as possible downstairs? That's why they are drugged."

"How does this make you feel?"

She stared into his face. He was a different Papa Jay than she remembered. When he took her, he had one face and when she woke up, he had another one. This new face plain, uninspired. It made him easier to talk to, since it wasn't as threatening.

She shrugged one of her shoulders. "I don't care."

"About?"

"About them."

"Why?"

She shrugged the other shoulder. "They are not me."

This made him smile. He showed her his wall of teeth, threw back his head and laughed.

"What do you care about?"

"Ballet."

"Anything else?"

"No. So if you let me do that…"

He waved her away. "I get it, I get it. Let me think and see what I can do."

She went to say more but stopped herself. It did no good to press. She went back to her room, got under the covers, and shut her eyes. In the darkness, she could see these girls rattling in their cages, calling out for her to help.

But she could not help them.

She could only help herself.

This made her smile too, the first real one in a long time.

## 4

GRACIE SURPRISED HERSELF WITH THE LIES SHE created to the girls in the basement. She spoke of a bad man after them (start with fear) and how her grandfather (who she called the Savior) rescued them before a worse destiny occurred. The cages were for their own safety too. The Savior couldn't trust them not to escape and the cages were honestly not so bad. Many of these girls were runaways living on the street. Here they had a bed (more like a piece of foam and a thin pillow) and they were injected with needles to help them sleep. They were fed (which wasn't a guarantee on the streets) and awaiting a new home. Gracie made up tall-tales about very rich men that would hire them to clean their houses, but they would be able to live in these houses too. They would have their own room with a soft bed and three meals a day. With this nugget, the girls began to perk up. She could hear them whispering dreams about the kind of men who would take them in and maybe they could fall in love with these men and get married.

When a girl would leave the basement, the rest all cheered. And the girl would smile so big—the fool. Gracie had been good at lying before. She duped her parents easily, although there wasn't too much to lie about. Most of it revolved around her eating habits, since she kept her calories to a minimum. "Lean like a whip," was how her dance teacher described their ideal bodies. So, she took to chewing her food more until the bites were pulverized and her jaw too tired to do any more work.

Papa Jay certainly noticed the difference in the girl's attitudes. Even though they were drugged, the atmosphere in the basement was light and full of positive energy—all due to Gracie.

"I'm impressed," he said, cutting into a steak one night. She hated meat but chewed little bites to keep him impressed. "You did exactly what you said you would do."

"So does that mean...?"

"You don't ask about your mother ever, or your father, your brother...?"

She took a sip of Mexican cola that he had bought for her. "Why should I?"

"I'm aware you miss them."

She swallowed a lump of sinew. "It was a different life."

She had rehearsed what she would say to him if this subject arose. If she carried on about missing her family, he'd think her weak. And it wasn't much of a lie. She missed parts of her life from New York City, obviously ballet, but other than that, she didn't really have friends and never thought about her family when she wasn't with them. When her father initially got sick, she mourned that he could die. It was as if she already said goodbye.

As for her brother, he was a clown. Never-ending fart jokes and he always smelled like beans. Her mother was likely the closest person to her, but they never really talked. Neither really knew who the other one was. Part of that was Gracie's fault—she was a hard nut to crack. But it was as if her mother considered it too difficult a hurdle and never tried. She was certain her mother missed her. Likely she spent her days in tears, and for that, Gracie felt bad. But in terms of missing her family, they were not her prime thought.

"I spoke with a woman," Gable said, his incisors tearing at a piece of red steak. "She owns a studio...a ballet studio."

Gracie lit up. It was as if she'd been idle and now she was plugged in.

"She is the aunt of one of my bodyguards, the larger one you call Mountain."

She liked Mountain. He was quiet and kind, for a murderer. She knew he'd killed people before and found that intriguing. He stood outside her room all night while she slept and she could hear him breathing. He breathed loud, his massive body sounding like a huge gust of wind when he'd exhale. It calmed her and put her to sleep each night.

So this became how each day Mountain would take her to his Aunt Valeria's studio. They drove in a car with black windows so she couldn't see out. She knew she was in Mexico but might as well have been anywhere. Sometimes Mountain would play music and hum along.

Valeria's studio was up a skinny flight of stairs on a

second floor that looked out over a dead-end street. She couldn't see people, only a mangy dog that rooted through a garbage can, the dog's nipples pink and flapping. Valeria was an older woman but not elderly. She stood straight as if a string connected her to the ceiling, her hair pushed back into a fierce bun with gray roots like lightning bolts toward her forehead. She wore so much makeup, Gracie had no idea what she actually looked like. Maybe that was the point so she couldn't be easily identified. She wore a floral wrap, practically see-through, her nails and toes painted crimson. It made Gracie miss her own polish.

"So, you're a dancer," Valeria said, not as a question. "We'll see about that."

She gave a huff, clearly unhappy with this arrangement. Gracie wondered what Papa Jay had done to get her to agree. Did he threaten her? Or was she simply doing a favor since Mountain was employed by her grandfather? She decided it wasn't her business.

Valeria was a stickler, even more so than her last teacher. By the end of the first day, Gracie's toes bled and she was in love. She went home dreaming about Valeria, the woman shouting at her to perform. Pure bliss.

Each day, nothing was spoken between them except for ballet. Gracie would get her hour lesson, Valeria never giving her a second overtime. She wasn't a warm woman, her eyes sad. Gracie imagined her life. Was she under a cartel's thumb? Gracie thought of the news she'd see on TV with the bodies hung from lampposts. She decided Valeria had lost someone she loved this way.

Over time, Gracie improved. What had caused her

title back in the States, no longer plagued. She never had the lead role before but now was certain she would at home. At night, she'd perform for the girls, an entirely new bunch since all the old ones had been replaced. They were in awe of her abilities but had nothing to compare it to. Still, she knew she was doing well.

"I'm getting better?" she asked Valeria one rainy day. The season had changed, no longer brutally hot but still sticky. The rain hit against the window like pellets.

Valeria gave the slightest shrug. "You are decent."

She leaped so much that day she bled more than usual. One toenail had ripped off, hanging for dear life. The pain made her feel alive.

"How can I get better?"

In her room, she'd practice. For the girls, she'd practice. And then the lessons. Every day was divided into ballet, nothing else. And she was good, she knew that. But great?

"Sometimes," Valeria began, watching the rain. She folded her arms, a frown developing. "We get to what we think is perfection, but it is not perfection."

Gracie had no clue what that meant. She launched into a diatribe about the girls in her ballet class back home and how she was sure to get the lead. She made the mistake of saying, "when I return."

Valeria's eyes shot over, bulging with bloodshot veins. Then she caught herself, as if she'd revealed too much.

"What?" Gracie asked. This was the most they had spoken.

"Nothing. Again," Valeria said, clapping her hands.

"I'm not ever going home, am I?" Gracie asked. She couldn't help but cry. She hadn't cried since she'd been taken and maybe it was because it had all been bottled up, or that she'd never vocalized her penance before. This was her life forever, at least for years. She could dance for the girls in the basement, but what did it matter if they would just be replaced? She could dance for Valeria, but she would never truly perform again. And this tragedy is what would keep her from becoming truly great. Because she wouldn't have the desire.

Dancing fed her soul, but the act of performance is what she lived for. To remove that too cruel a punishment. Papa Jay let her come to this studio, but he'd never allow anything more. This and the basement the only space to display her talents. So what was the purpose of it all, if no one would really see? If she'd never receive her standing ovation?

She stopped dancing for the girls. At first, they asked for it but soon forgot. She gave up on lifting their spirits and the basement became entrenched in a sad fog. No longer did she make up stories about rich men that may fall in love with these girls. Their future would only be worse, and in her heart, she knew many would wind up dead once they weren't required to perform in their own way.

She still went to ballet class but her enthusiasm had waned. One day she refused to dance and she and Valeria just sat in silence until Mountain came to take her back. This repeated for many days to the point that Valeria left her in the room while she took the hour to clean the rest of the studio. Gracie watched the mangy dog outside the window in the alleyway. It had become thin to the point of grotesque, all of its bones on display. The next day when it didn't show up, she cried.

She hated her weakness but couldn't help it. She thought of taking her life. Searching for anything that could wound, her eyes spied a nailfile left on a table. She ran it across her wrists as Valeria entered with a broom.

"It won't work, child," she said, whipping the nail-file out of her hands.

"I don't care."

"Yes, it seems you don't care about anything."

"This is it," Gracie said, rubbing her eyes as more tears fell. "This studio, and you, and Mountain, and then back to the house. Every day is the same."

"You want me to feel bad for you?" Valeria asked, sucking at her teeth. "Because I won't."

"Why?"

"You still have it better than most, foolish little white girl. You've been given everything, so you expect it. Well, the world doesn't work that way. We rise and we fall. Most have never gotten as high as you."

"Why do you do this for my grandfather?"

Valeria slapped her across the face harder than she'd ever been hit before. Her face throbbed as she held onto her cheek.

"You want me dead?" Valeria asked, shaking. "Is that what you want?"

"Is that what he does?"

Valeria gave her a knowing look. Gracie felt ashamed for asking. Papa Jay was a very bad man and she could tell herself otherwise to hide the truth but it'd be for naught. It was at that moment she had the revelation that her only choice was to join him. She could learn his business; she could grow into his number two. She heard him speak of past "number twos" before. The walls were thin in the house and he mentioned a man called The Doctor, who was his current number two and working from a different house. She didn't know if it was other girls he managed or something unsavory, but it didn't matter to her. She would be successful at whatever she put her mind to and if it wouldn't be ballet, such was life.

"Miss," she says, batting her wet eyes.

"Yes?"

"Don't fucking hit me again."

Valeria's eyebrows rose and she scratched at a mole on her neck nervously.

"I'm not someone to be fucked with."

With that Gracie marched out of the studio, waiting for Mountain on the skinny staircase. The next day, she swore she would dance again for Valeria, just not with all her heart.

## 5

Once Gracie had the revelation that it was better to join Papa Jay, rather than try to beat him, a lightness took hold. Prior, her shoulders were oppressed as if two heavy birds had set up perch. There was no use in attempting to be "good" anymore. Where had being good gotten her? She'd be kidnapped by an employer of her grandfather only to be purloined off on him. If this was all from being good, she may as well try being bad.

"Papa," she said, as he sat smoking a cigar with a glass of Scotch. It was nighttime, very late and past her bedtime, except she didn't really have a bedtime. She'd gotten in the habit of calling him Papa in a cutesy way and he never corrected.

"Yes?"

He seemed tired, or rather, more exhausted than normal. He was an old man and the last few years had done a number. He eyes squinted so much they were barely open.

"I want to join the business."

He rubbed those barely open eyes. "What business?"

She cackled enough for him to flinch. Had she gone mad? Quite. But at the same time, she was more lucid than ever. She had seen him on the news where a reporter spoke about his Desire Card, a one-way ticket that promised "Any wish fulfilled for the right price." Rich people contacted him to get them whatever they wanted, at least back in the States. Here in Mexico, he pawned off street girls for whoever paid top dollar. She could help.

"The girls..." The word felt alien on her tongue, sizzling as if the devil had been made aware of her plunge. "You get them off the street."

"I don't think you should—"

She threw her arms up. "Oh Papa, I don't care. Really. You don't have to talk to me like I'm a child."

"You are a child."

She held up a finger. "Only in size."

He laughed at that.

"You sell these girls, right?" she continued.

"Yes."

"Well, what if you could get better girls?"

He blinked as if he'd awoken from a strange dream. "What are you getting at?"

She thought about this carefully all night. It reminded her of a presentation she once did in school. The teacher had told her to lead with facts so that was what she'd do.

"These girls are from the streets. They do drugs, they don't eat, they are not healthy. But wouldn't your men want a...better girl?"

"And by better girl...?"

"There are resorts not far from here in other towns, right? Wealthy families come with their daughters..." She was talking so fast, she could hardly keep up. Excitement spilling off her tongue. She hadn't been excited in so long and she could feel it in her beating heart. "I could get close to these girls. Hang out at the resorts, no one will blink at me. I could lure them to—"

He raised his palm. "That is nefarious."

"I don't know that word."

"This is why you are still a child."

"I'm sure a lot of people don't know that word. Most adults are pretty stupid."

"*Touché.* Okay, first, I applaud your hustle. You are in a piss poor situation and trying to make the most of it. You don't complain anymore and keep your head down. I admire that."

"Thank you."

"My organization is always thinking of new ways to grow, so your ideas have value. Except the problem with it is that girls from fancy families have parents who will miss them. Police are called. An American goes missing here and it's a national news story. The girls on the streets have no one who cares."

Gracie chewed her lip. "What if I helped with the girls on the street? I can do the same. Befriend them, lure them here."

"That involves you being out on the streets as well."

"I know. I...dancing isn't enough. I want to contribute."

Papa Jay took a sniff of his drink and swirled some in his mouth. "What if I called on you to do odd jobs? Anything needed. A starter agent? Then we see how it goes."

Her eyes got big. "I'll do anything."

"I believe you." He stroked his new chin. "I really do."

Odd jobs kept her busy. She continued dancing for one-hour a day in the mornings, but afternoons and sometimes nights were devoted to whatever Papa Jay had for her. It ranged from cleaning the cages of the girls (disgusting) to learning how to use the needles to drug them. His operatives Brando and Astaire were being called on for more business outside of the house, and Mountain and the other bodyguard were there to simply guard her body, so Gracie became her grandfather's go-to for any quick business needed. In addition to overseeing the girls in the basement, she was tested as an abductor too. In the past, Brando or Astaire just grabbed a girl in the night and threw her in a van, but this didn't always work. Sometimes the girl fought back, sometimes they screamed before they were drugged. It was a messy way to go about it, so they tried having Gracie sit in the back of the van with doors open. When a street girl would pass by, Gracie would draw them in by asking a question. Usually, she went with asking if they wanted to make some money in Spanish and the girls, at least, would stop and listen. Most of them haven't been properly fed in weeks, maybe months, and saw this sweet little *gringo* girl in a black SUV. She'd smile a pearly smile at them and they'd be hooked. They'd lean in closer and then out of the shadows, Brando or Astaire would stab them in the neck with the needle. It was a success.

"Don't think I haven't seen how well you're doing," Papa Jay said. He'd been away from the house more and more, leading her to believe that his business had been expanding. He spoke sometimes of a man called The Doctor, which ran the business from a different location. All signs pointed to the new Card burgeoning beyond street girls.

"I'm good at it," Gracie declared. She was turning twelve and had almost spent two years in Mexico. Her Spanish was improving and she wore her hair slick and pulled back. She'd lay out on the back lawn to develop as much of a tan as possible. She wanted to be seen as an equal and not as a *gringo*. It only helped her bring in more girls.

"I might have a new job for you," he said, ashing his cigar. She swallowed hard, her chest booming.

She was right that the business was booming. All the clients were pleased with their girls and now Papa Jay wanted to deliver more of a "package." The goal was to give his clients the experience of a party. The Doctor had been spending his time making inroads in the drug, and specifically, cocaine trade. *Did she know what cocaine was?* Papa Jay asked. She cocked her head to the side, like, duh. Even though she didn't quite understand, she knew it was white and looked like powder and made people go wild. What more was there to know? Anyway, to give the clients an experience, Papa Jay wanted drugs to go with the girls. Sure, the clients could get these drugs separately, but that was not always so easy. Since the cartels ran the drug trade, a client that didn't have those connections was fucked. So, if the girls could arrive with enough cocaine for a party, then that was a bonus.

"Makes sense," Gracie said.

"But here's the rub. We can't give the girls the cocaine, they'll just do it themselves, and a lot of the clients like the girls to arrive on their own. It gives the illusion that this is what the girls want to do, not that they are being sold."

"You need someone to bring the girls in with the cocaine," Gracie said, clearing her throat.

Papa Jay tapped his nose. "Precisely. We would have Brando or Astaire or even Mountain as you call him drive you to the client's house. He would be watching the entire time and you would deliver the girl and the cocaine in a nice box or something like that. You see, someone like Mountain arrives at their door, it can be threatening. But with you..."

"I understand. I want Mountain."

"Of course. Nothing could happen to you. Mountain will see to that. And for your troubles..." He ashed again into an ashtray. "You will move up in my organization to trainee status. This is a big deal, Gracie."

Her teeth were chattering. She quieted them. "I know."

"Then it is done."

So Gracie grew into a thirteen-year-old, dancing like always in the mornings and delivering girls and drugs usually at night. The clients called her *Muñeca*, since she was so small. The cocaine was put in the box with a bow and a new Desire Card (*Tarjeta de Deseo*) to chop it up. She'd lead the shaking girl by the arm, who had just woken up from a slumber, to the client's door and ring the bell. When they opened the door, she'd present the girl along with the tiny box, never saying a word. She'd speak with her eyes. Those eyes told the clients she would never enter into their houses, even if that was a desire of theirs, and there was no bargaining. They would, in turn, hand over an envelope with the money. Transactions were to always be paid with bills, so they could avoid the banks. Sometimes the men would try and cajole her with promises of swimming pools and candies, but she would stare into their souls and tell them (politely) no.

Of course, incidents occurred. The men, and the occasional woman clients, were wealthy, but not *so* wealthy that they could procure their own desires without help. Still, they lived in a world where whatever they wanted, they found a way to obtain. As Gracie, or *Muñeca*, came to be known throughout the city, she sparked a fancy in a few. As she grew up, they took one look at the strung-out girl being delivered to them and then healthy Gracie, and refused to let her leave. Mountain always came to her rescue, barreling out of the SUV and grabbing the client by the neck. Most of the time, the client was so high that they didn't know what was going on and solely had the mindset of fucking in their brain. Gracie was never harmed, so she never thought twice about stopping. Also, the years of ballet had made her strong. Let one of the clients try something without Mountain around, she'd get them in the balls and bring them to the ground.

After four years in Mexico, her grandfather approached her about becoming an operative.

"What does it involve?"

She had taken up smoking, little *cigarillos* that she'd roll herself, her fingers stained yellow. It squelched her appetite and kept her stick thin. The baby fat had melted off her cheeks, replaced with cheekbones any model would kill for. The clients no longer called her *Muñeca*.

"I'm thinking about what you said to me when you started."

She sucked hard, squeezing her cheeks.

"Hard to believe but we're running out of street girls. We've done the city a service."

He let out one solitary bark of a laugh.

"What if you checked out a resort?"

Their area was landlocked so it didn't have the beach resorts like those on the coast. But still, families came to swim the pools, often ones looking for a cheaper vacation. The benefit of this was that the wealthier parents would have a better chance of hiring someone adept at tracking their daughter down. These middle-class families would rely on the police, who were corrupt and easily paid off. As long as they didn't do it too often, these girls would simply become lost and blamed for venturing out of their resort area and into the streets.

"The key is getting them off the property," he said. "Then we're golden. I have a client in particular, who will pay top dollar. In fact, this was his request. An American."

She pictured this girl: Bayleigh, or McKayla, or some other variation of two names smushed together. Midwestern. She'd chew bubble gum like a cow and wrap the gum around her finger. She'd be looking to rebel.

Gracie agreed and staked out the resorts. No one blinked at her walking in, assuming she was part of a family like everyone else. She'd ask for virgin daiquiris and flirt with the bartender to put in a splash of alcohol, then roam. Mountain waited outside in the SUV with headphones and she could spend hours away. At first, the thrill of normalcy overwhelmed. She could do anything. Join the kids for games. Go to a buffet. A dance party. But she hadn't socialized like that in so long, she found herself tongued tied with what to say. So she started lounging at the pool, sipping daiquiris, waiting for a girl to approach her. It would be better that way. They would only take one girl, at least for a good length of time. It had to be the right girl.

A few weeks into her hunt, she was sunning when two pale legs stood before her in a one-piece bathing suit with rainbows. The girl wore jellies and had a scab on her knee. As Gracie's eyes traveled up, she took in her lip gloss, braces, a smattering of freckles, and long blonde hair (blonde was a request from the client, since it was rare).

"Hi!" Gracie said. Smile big, speak in exclamation points. "I'm Valeria."

Her ballet instructor was the first name that popped into her head. "Everyone calls me Val," she said, with a flip of her hair.

"I like your bathing suit," the girl said, pointing and then covering her own in embarrassment. "I'm Adele."

"Thanks, my grandfather got it for me," Gracie said. She knew it was best not to veer too far from the truth when lying. Papa Jay had bought it for her and spent a lot of money as a gift for the work she was about to do. It was yellow like a canary and two-piece. Gracie noticed how even Mountain couldn't keep his eyes off of her with it on.

"My folks and brother are being sooo annoying," Adele said, crossing her thin arms. "They've barely left the buffet the whole time."

"Mine are so busy with business that they just left me by the pool. I'm bored."

"Me too, this place is the worst."

Gracie looked around. Children splashing in the water. Women sunning and men with sunglasses and colorful drinks. Everyone reddened and buzzed from the sun.

"I have a joint," Gracie said.

Adele's eyes lit up. A few minutes later, they were walking behind the hotel's restaurant where an air vent spit steam. Gracie leaned against a wall and lit the joint, taking an extra-long suck. She passed it over.

"I've only done it once," Adele said, inhaling and coughing immediately.

"Coughing is good. Your lungs are getting used to it."

Once high, Adele wouldn't stop talking. She was from Miami and her father worked in business, although she didn't really know what he did. They had a large white house overlooking the ocean and her parents threw parties all the time. Her dad had some business deal down here so they decided on a vacation, even though the resort wasn't up to the places they usually booked. Adele bogarted the joint but Gracie didn't care. The point was to get the girl wasted, not her.

"Have you been out of the hotel?" Gracie asked, motioning for Adele to continue inhaling.

"No. (cough). I (cough) heard it was kinda sketch."

"Nah, that's just what the hotel says so you spend all your money here."

"It's all inclusive."

"Still, all the tips. Anyway, there's like this super

cool place down the road that plays awesome music where we can go dance. Some older boys hang out there."

Adele's eyes got wide and she nibbled her lip.

"I went last night. No one even noticed I was gone. I made out with this boy from town. He had bedroom eyes."

"What's that?"

"Wanna go?"

Gracie grabbed Adele's arm and started to yank her but Adele stayed in place.

"I don't want to get in trouble."

"You said your family hasn't left the buffet table, so they won't even know you're gone. This place is so big too, you can make an excuse you were anywhere. Seriously, it's right down the road."

A long line of sweat dripped from Adele's temple.

"C'mon, it'll be fun. They'll serve us too. I tried tequila last night."

"Oh, how did it taste?"

"It burned, but in like a good way."

Gracie yanked her again, growing impatient. "C'mon."

Adele was less hesitant this time. There was a back gate behind the restaurant (which Gracie knew about in advance) that Gracie unlatched and the two girls giggled as they ran down a steep road. The van was parked blocks away, so no cameras might eye it, and Gracie felt her heart thrumming into her chest as she directed Adele further away from safety. Adele was telling a story about her brother that didn't make much sense. They turned down an alleyway and then another, and all Gracie could think about was that this dumb girl wouldn't shut the fuck up. Now Adele was talking about her favorite things. She loved caramel but hated chocolate. She liked this boy back home with the unfortunate name of Newt (?) but wasn't sure if he liked her. Once they touched hands at the cafeteria line on Taco Tuesday and she told him she was going to Mexico. Gracie tuned her out. Was this how Americans always were? How she was? So selfish, the world revolving around them? She was disgusted by this Adele and decided the girl deserved whatever befell her for being so clueless and gullible.

"Is it close?" Adele asked. "I don't hear any music."

The van sat puttering on the curb spitting black exhaust from its pipe. One of the doors was cracked open, an eye peering through. Gracie knew it was Brando or Astaire. Both of them so weird, she barely spoke to them, but they had fast hands.

"Hmm," Gracie said, flexing her best acting muscles. "I could've sworn it was down this way. Let me fix my flip flop."

Gracie directed Adele toward the van, leaning against it while she pretended to remove a pebble from between her toes.

"What's going on?" Adele asked. The girl blinked hard. Either the pot was wearing off, or had just really kicked in.

"Nothing, don't be weird."

"You're being..."

Adele couldn't finish because the van doors flung open and from out of the darkness a masked face of an old movie star appeared. Adele let out the tiniest scream that became engulfed when Brando (or maybe it was Astaire, Gracie always mixed them up) clamped his hand over the girl's mouth and whisked her inside.

Two scared eyes appeared in the dark, pleading with Gracie for help. But Gracie simply closed the doors and tapped the van so the driver (either Brando or Astaire) could take off. The driver floored it and the van shot down the block before turning the corner.

Gracie pulled the remnants of the joint from her pocket and took a cool puff.

Now that the mission had been completed, she could finally relax.

6

ADELE WASN'T KEPT IN THE BASEMENT FOR LONG,
since she was in demand from Papa Jay's clients. Gracie
duct-taped her mouth and delivered her personally to a
man with the largest belly and largest house she'd ever
seen. It had multiple pools and a fountain with dolphin
sculptures, a zillion TVs and a sauna. The man had
cocaine dusting his face and Adele was acting over-
dramatic, mewling and weeping through the duct-tape.

"This is a palace," Gracie told her. "Just don't piss
him off."

Mountain had been waiting to drive her back.
When she got in the car, he asked how it went.
Normally he was quiet, never speaking much.

Gracie lowered the window and lit a cigarette.
She'd recently been able to make Os. "Fine."

"Her case made the papers," he said, and tossed
back a newspaper. Her Spanish had gotten so good that
she could read it without any help. On the front page,
Adele's class photo. She was folding her arms and
smiling at the world.

"What does Papa think?"

Mountain shrugged one shoulder.

When she returned home, Papa Jay waited with a lit cigar and a glass of port. His nightly ritual. They discussed the drop, which Gracie said went well and the newspaper article. Papa Jay didn't seem upset, rather more alive than he'd been in a long time. She'd watched her grandfather age these past few years. Now he had a newfound vitality.

"You think it'll be an issue?" she asked.

"Who's to say? We'll know when we know."

For a while, the case stayed in the papers but soon moved from the front page to a later section. Gracie had been careful enough to be out of line of any cameras, so there was no connection back to her. The police didn't seem to make much headway either, even though the parents were vocal. She saw them on the news once. The mother frighteningly thin, a ball of nerves. The father with a mean smirk. He said little.

But then came word that the man they sold Adele to had been robbed. She heard Papa Jay shouting about it over the phone. Adele had been discovered in the man's safe room and the man had been tortured. They cut off his nose. She imagined this man, nose-less, when she went to bed. Then she heard gunfire.

Looking out her window at the back lawn, men were descending on the house. They had big guns that weighed heavy in their hands. They shot up the back door and either Brando or Astaire (she could never tell them apart). The one still alive fired back, leaping at these men from the top of the staircase. She was barefoot and had no time to grab her shoes. She ran to Papa Jay's room, but his window was wide open. From out of it, she could see him fleeing into the night, without her. She felt arms wrap around her, and tried to struggle, until she saw it was Mountain.

"The girl's father," Mountain whispered in her ear. "He knows. Wants revenge. The client told on us."

She was impressed at how well Mountain's English had improved since she arrived. Even though they didn't speak to each other much, he was always listening.

"I'm getting you out of here," he said, moving toward the door.

"But Papa Jay?"

"He left you. He left us. He's a coward."

"I love you," she said, because she was actually scared and she truly did.

He shielded her as he barreled out of the door. They flew past Brando or Astaire, who got one in the gut and tumbled over the balcony to his death. Mountain took one bullet in the arm and in his leg, but he still protected her as he fled through the busted door. She screamed through a sea of bullets until they reached a car. Mountain threw her inside and then jumped in and gunned the gas. The back window shattered from the impact of more bullets, but they flew away and soon reached a road where they heard bullets no more.

He took her to Valeria's house. She lived over the studio and had been woken up. In the middle of the night, she had cold cream all over her face and no hair. She'd always worn a wig and for some reason this made Gracie cry.

Mountain and his aunt yelled at each other in Spanish. His aunt was not pleased that he brought the girl there, but Mountain said there was nowhere else to go. He wanted to get her to America, back to her home. It wasn't safe for her to stay. Valeria refused to spend a dime on the girl, but Mountain said that he would. He produced a fat stack of money for Valeria to take the girl to the airport. He said that they would be looking for him and it would be suicide if he went.

"She is a child," he said, but Valeria slapped him. Finally, she relented and put on a wig and a housecoat and slippers. She would call a cab. That was the most she would do.

When the cab arrived, Mountain took her down to the street. It was the middle of the night and only alley cats slinked around. Someone was yelling in the distance. Gracie felt a chill.

"What will happen to you?" she asked.

Mountain wouldn't look at her. He went to put her in a cab.

Gracie hadn't had a hug since she'd been kidnapped. Papa Jay would never. But Mountain leaned down and gave her a crushing hug that squeezed her bones. She swore she could see a tear in his eye.

"I'm sorry," he said, and shoved her in the cab. She spun around as the cab drove away and he stalked off into the night. She knew he was marked for death. If not tonight, then soon. Valeria probably as well. Everyone she'd come in contact with since she arrived, except for Papa Jay. He was a slippery eel and he'd manage to make it out of this unscathed.

She reached the airport after many miles. She had no ID on her, but enough money to bribe. She gave over the whole stack of bills and by the morning, was on a flight bound to Mexico City and then another to JFK.

She didn't have to worry about getting through

security when she got back to the States. She was recognized right away by the gate agent. Even though it'd been almost five years since she'd been taken, Gracie Stockton's case was national news. They kept her in a room until her mother, a much older, much weathered version of her mother came to bring her home. When her father didn't show up too, she knew he had passed.

But it had been a long last few days—last few years really—and she didn't have it in her to care. When she got back to her bedroom that looked like a little girl's room belonging to someone else, all she wanted to do was sleep. She closed the door on her mother and did just that for days on end, seasons even, until she woke up to a blizzard of snow, the likes of which she hadn't seen since she was a child. And it was glorious.

## 7

THE PICTURES IN MOTION DISSOLVE ON THE ceiling of the hut. On the back of William Clark's tongue, the taste of rot. He tries to vomit a little but nothing comes up. His body exhausted, as if he'd traveled a long distance without any sleep. For a moment, he's not in the jungle, his mind still in Mexico. But the old, old woman resurfaces across from him. Her crinkly gray hair still covers her face. All he can see is a nose poking through. And the essence of eyes. Although, as he looks closer, she doesn't seem to have irises, only two fat black pupils making up her sockets. It's the first instance he really wonders if she is of this world. If he even is on this planet, or if he's been transported somewhere far away in the stars?

She points a quivering finger with a long fingernail in his direction. "Your granddaughter... Do you see what you've done?"

"I helped raise her."

The old woman lets out a laugh that doesn't seem to end. In her mouth, teeth so tiny, like that of a child.

"It's a testament to Gracie," he says. "She's a survivor. Anything else in her life will be surmountable. That is a gift."

"If those are your gifts..."

"I showed her what the world is. That it's cruel. Evil. It's a lesson in hard knocks." He lets out a cough that's ringed with cruel blood that dribbles down his chin. "We all experience it at some point. Yet we want to protect children. Why? The biggest cruelty out there is letting a child think that the world is full of love. It's best not to fight the wave and ride the current."

"You speak of love—"

"I speak of the absence of love."

"You have never had true love."

"You say that as a statement."

"Because it is true."

"You are thinking of my wife? Vivienne? She's like me, a block of ice. She could probably admit, like I would, that she was in love with moments. The birth of our children, our grandchildren."

The old woman shakes her finger. "Who you also never loved."

"Why, because I took Gracie? One could say I freed her."

The old woman blows a raspberry. "From what?"

"Ennui. The plight of a rich white Upper East Side girl from New York City. She was living in ignorance."

The old woman taps her whiskered chin. "So, you kidnapped other girls and sold them off to prove that the world is evil to her?"

"No, that was a bonus. I did it for money."

"Yes," the old woman hisses. "The root of it all."

"Isn't that trite? A poor cliché. Money is necessary

for societies not to descend into chaos. It gets us out of bed every day."

"Maybe for you...?"

"Even here, in this jungle, or wherever we are, you must barter. You have to give objects value."

"No, I have ascended beyond that. Earthly possessions mean nothing to me."

"A-ha," he says, snapping until his arthritis causes him to wince. "So, we are on Earth?"

"What makes you think we are not?"

"Your...everything. The fact that I had a window into the past. How do you explain that?"

"I am one with the Earth. I know its secrets. How to unlock its full potential."

"Gobbledygook, that's what you speak. I've entered a funhouse. I'm in my dreams, yes, I...I must've fallen, hit my head. And so, this hut appeared."

The old woman stomps over. She slices his cheeks with a swipe of her fingernails like a cat.

"What the...?"

"The flesh burns," she says, sucking on the back of her tongue. "This is not a dream."

He lunges at her. The bodyguard swoops in to block. He gets a look at a face, like a mirror into time. His own reflection staring back, but forty years ago, when the Desire Card was a baby.

Drool seeps from the old woman's lips. "This is your reckoning. Do you understand me?"

"Yes, the ghost of Christmas past visited. What's next, my future?"

"Your daughter's."

"Helene?"

"Although, what I will show you has already happened. That is how time works here."

"Where?"

She gestures to her bodyguard who brings another drink over. The color different, this one bluer, like the ocean. He takes a sip and dives in.

"You spoke of good and evil before?" she says.

"You gonna tell me you are good and I am evil? You are God and I'm the devil?"

"It's not as simple as that," they both say at the same time. He is stunned but she smirks.

"There's a balance in everyone. Sometimes the scale tips."

"So that's your diagnosis? I tipped?"

A gust of wind blows through the hut's opening. Either the old woman shakes her head, or the wind does it for her.

"I am searching for where *it* began—"

"What?"

"If it even started with you."

He gulps. "You mean, my...tendencies?"

The wind swirls around. "Your demon."

Up on the ceiling Helene appears. His daughter, but different than how he remembers. Like a sock rung out in the wash. She's gaunt, her cheeks caving inward, her hair blindingly white. Her eyes soulless. This is what he did to her when he took her child away for five years. He destroyed everything that made her shine.

"Dad?" she asks, her eyes narrowing.

And then, as if she wakes from her stupor, a smile flashes. She's startled by it at first, still getting used to the gesture. But it's okay now. Her daughter is home.

She's in her room, even though she barely leaves her room, but at least she is safe.

She's alive.

"For now," the old woman says, her tongue slithering through her lips, forked in two.

8

GRACIE HAS BARELY LEFT HER BEDROOM SINCE SHE
returned home. Helene becoming concerned. At first,
Helene treaded lightly. Set her daughter up with a therapist but Gracie refused to leave the house. Then an
online therapist, but Gracie didn't want to turn on the
computer. She wanted to sleep and watch TV. She ate
cans of tuna fish and had her own bathroom, so she was
able to exist entirely in her confined space. Fall turned
to a very cold winter and Helene became stuck inside
too. Both of them breathing the same air, but miles
apart.

Her ex-husband Harrison had succumbed to
complications from his liver transplant a few years back.
Before Gracie had been taken by her father, they devel-
oped a cordial relationship. He had the kids every other
weekend and was trying to be a good parent, more than
he did when they were together. She began dating
Peter, a polar opposite from Harrison, a good man who
devoted his time to causes and volunteerism. He would
hold her hand. He would kiss her ear. He was doting in

a way she always wanted Harrison to be but knew he didn't have it in him. Yet Gracie's disappearance was too much for Peter to take on. Helene took out her anger and frustration on him, and after a year of abuse, he left.

It was easier without him around. The first year she went gung-ho into attempting to find Gracie. She exhausted every single contact that might be connected to her father, but Jay had the means to vanish wherever he pleased and the world was a very big place. After Peter left, she took to her bedroom (like daughter, like mother). She slept. For in her dreams sometimes Gracie still was with her. Her son Brenton was a senior in high school and busy enough not to care about his mother's comings and goings. There were days he didn't even notice she was holed up for hours on end. Their relationship had become strained and he couldn't wait to get to college to be away from her. His family that only seemed to bring doom into his life. Now he was at William & Mary on a soccer scholarship and called maybe once a month, even after Gracie returned home.

In some ways she deserved this penance. She'd been blind to the moral decline of both her father and ex-husband. She had to have known their treachery, especially her father. All these years, she couldn't have been that ignorant. She didn't know what was worse.

Now that Gracie was back, she'd taken up a part time position at UNESCO where she used to work when the kids were younger. She spent mornings there and was home by the time Gracie woke up. She'd open a can of tuna fish, leave it outside of her door, and pick it back up when Gracie finished.

She made a deal with Gracie that she wouldn't have

to return to school immediately, or even get tutored until she acclimated enough back to her surroundings. But come spring semester, Gracie would have no choice. Now it was December, meaning Gracie had a few scant weeks to get herself in order. Today Helene would have a long talk with her. Gracie was good at currying favor and Helene had become weak. She'd need to put her foot down.

"Gracie?" she asked, knocking on the door with a can of Chicken of the Sea in hand.

"Just leave it outside," came a murmur from under the crack.

"I need to have a word with you."

She tried the door, but it was locked. After debating on whether or not to remove the lock earlier, she had decided against it. She would never be her mother, who alternated between exacting control and being an ice block.

"Please, Gracie...it won't take long."

Silence passed and she was about to give up when the door unlocked and swung open. Gracie sat perched on her canopy bed, thin to the point of grotesque (like mother, like daughter). The room smelled clogged with cigarette smoke, or vape Helene guessed. The windows sealed shut, the heater spitting steam. Helene pulled the chair from under the desk and sat down.

Gracie had the look of oversleep, something Helene knew all too well. A foggy glaze issuing from her eyes. Those eyes bugged for Helene to speak.

"We need to talk about school."

Gracie gave a flip of her hair as a response.

"You're not even fifteen, you have to go back to school. The semester starts in..."

"Mother," Gracie said, like a weapon. "Don't you understand...?"

Helene's sigh seemed everlasting. "Understand what?"

"School is for... You don't know what I've been through."

*What we've all been through*, Helene thought. "Tell me."

Gracie reached out and Helene realized it was for the can of tuna. Helene looked for a can opener, but Gracie grabbed one already from her bedside. She opened the can and stuck a tiny fork in, chewed delicately.

"You wouldn't be able to handle it," Gracie said, with a cool smirk.

"What he did to you," Helene simmered.

"No." Gracie slammed the can of tuna down on her bedside table. "I am *not* a victim. Do you hear me?"

Her daughter was thundering, a lightning bolt vein appearing on her temple.

Helene held up her palms. "Of course, of course."

"It's an American way. Oh, I'm the victim. Boo hoo. I don't want anyone crying for me."

"Good, you shouldn't. Show that you can move on from this."

"Ha," Gracie said, and plucked her vape from under her bedsheets. She took a pineapple puff. "It's not a question of moving on. What am I moving on to?"

"Being a normal girl. Going to school, hanging out with friends, going on dates, college."

"I see, but the problem is that the path has been forked."

Helene got a chill when her daughter said, "forked."

"All of that is meaningless to me."

"You have to try."

Helene was tearing now, mostly out of exhaustion. If she just had a partner, this wouldn't be so difficult. There were too many decisions solely on her shoulders.

"For who? Who am I trying for?"

"For you. You have your whole life ahead of you and I promise... I really promise that all you went through will eventually get pushed further and further away."

"What if I don't want it to?"

"What do you mean?"

"I don't want to go back to being a stupid little girl. What I've seen, mother. Girls sold into sex slavery. People get shot and bleed out in front of me. That is the real world."

"No, that was a moment of time."

"I found it thrilling."

Gracie smiles now, one that makes Helene think of the devil. She's let the devil into her life before. She grew up in his embrace. It's in her DNA, her daughter's too.

"Don't say that."

"I'm more like Papa Jay than you think. He's a terrible man, but a genius at what he's good at."

Helene slapped her because she didn't know what else to do. She stood there shaking. Gracie didn't flinch. She licked at the dabble of blood building on her lip. She enjoyed her mother out of sorts.

"I'll go back to school," Gracie said, coolly. She got up off her bed, ushering her mother to the door. "But you will be out of my life. No more talks. No more heart-to-hearts. No therapy. You will leave me alone and I will stay out of your hair. That is the arrangement I'm offering."

"Gracie..."

Gracie raised her hand to slap Helene and Helene quivered. Laugher from deep inside of Gracie filled the room, swallowed Helene up, until she stepped out and let the door be closed in her face. It opened, and Helene had a moment of hope, but the can of tuna was chucked out only for the door to be slammed again.

"I'll feed myself," came a murmur from under the crack.

Helene picked up the can, slicing her finger, enough for it to bleed for days.

9

GRACIE WENT TO SCHOOL. SHE FOUND HER PEERS insipid, the schoolwork unchallenging. She spent most of time rolling *cigarillos* in the staircase. They treated her with kid gloves because of her trauma. So, she milked it. Then she had an idea. What if she laced those cigarettes with micro dosing mushrooms? When she wasn't in school, she'd roam Central Park at night. In the middle of the winter, the only souls in Central Park at night are the strange. She met a man in the Ramble who could get her anything she wanted for the right price. She flinched when she first heard him, the Card flashing in her mind. But then she realized it had become part of the lexicon, anyone who wanted to move product adopting its slogan.

She bought enough from him to put down an elephant, then upsold it by one thousand percent. Gracie went to the most prestigious prep school in New York City. Sultans sent their kids. Billionaires threw parties. And Gracie would be their connection for "Any wish fulfilled." Soon, the insipid girls became interesting. All it took was a few steady magic mushrooms in their diet. They say you can't get addicted to hallucinogens, but Gracie had the whole school in her fist, teachers included. She extended it beyond the confines of her brownstone school. There were a string of girls selling down West End Ave, the quietest part of the city. Full of the elderly with walkers. No one would suspect. Then business boomed even more when she switched to pain killers to rope the elderly in too. She had buyers all over the city. She had a card too, although it was plain white, nothing on it. Her girls weren't hard to find if you looked.

Once spring arrived, she set her sights on taking over Central Park—her girls spread out over the grass. Weed had been decriminalized and the park was filled with security, but very little police. She never had a problem. Pain killers led to cocaine, and she wondered if she was getting product from a vestige of what Papa Jay and The Doctor left behind. She'd gotten a peek into The Doctor's operation a few times, but found him a stressful person to be around. He was jittery and slick, he liked to call her Candie, pretending he'd forgotten her name. She wondered if he was dead, if they all were? Had Valeria and Mountain been killed for their treachery? She guessed that Papa Jay ran off somewhere, but did the violence he left behind spread through the town like a metastasizing cyst?

She believed he'd be proud of her. She was a survivor. And she was pulling in ten thousand a week at only fifteen. Her operation had tripled in three months since its inception. Summer was around the corner and she'd expand to other boroughs. She'd have her Bronx girls, her Queens girls, the Brooklyn bunch, but not

Staten Island because that shit was too far away. She got herself a tattoo that said *Muñeca*, along with a little doll across her back that looked like Chucky. Under her eyelids she had *Wish* and *Fulfilled* in blue ink. When Helene saw it first, she screamed. She threw a fit. But Gracie told her, "Mother, just let me go. Don't worry about me. Like, I'm not trying to hurt you." She'd picked up an accent, her own blend that mushed vowels. "But you being 'a mom' is like not what I need. So, if you wanna be chill then we can be cool. Like roommates."

"You never came back," Helene cried, because she was on pills that Gracie had given her. Spooky eyes stared at her daughter. "Something else did, it's not you."

"Go to bed."

Helene had scaled back her hours at UNESCO, taking to the bedroom again. It had become her lifeline. She'd seek it like an addict. And Gracie was pulling in so much money she didn't have to work.

"What you're doing..." Helene gasped. "The money that comes in."

Gracie yawned. "I'm fulfilling wishes, like I've been taught. And I can keep you swimming in wishes. You're swimming right now."

"My head," Helene said, pressing the heel of her hand against her forehead.

"I have something for that."

Gracie went into her room and came back with a red pill. Helene swallowed without even looking. She only wanted to numb, to escape this life. She couldn't be a mother anymore. She didn't have the energy. In her dreams, she was raised in the country. Not wealthy, just normal. A farm with many animals. She milked goats and tended to the chickens. Her parents were kind and simple, her world filled with bliss. Helene curled up in her bed clutching a pillow and whispered this dream. When she woke it was nighttime, a different night. She'd slept for a full day.

Rubbing her eyes, she stalked the halls. What had her daughter given her? Set to ream her child, she opened Gracie's bedroom door to find nothing. All of Gracie's little kid designs still dominated the walls, but her daughter had left. She knew it in her heart. She couldn't feel her presence anymore, and what scared her the most was that she was glad. When Gracie had been taken, Helene was eventually free to do whatever she wanted. And what she wanted was sleep.

She crawled back into bed and resurfaced on her imagined farm where the cut grass smelled like heaven and their world was never shaped by a Card.

## 10

WHEN HELENE HADN'T GOTTEN IN TOUCH WITH her mother for over a week, Vivienne decided to pay a visit. Pushing eighty, Vivienne had the life zapped out of her after the ordeal with her husband Jay, who became national news for the better part of a year once his alias had been revealed. She was hounded by reporters so much that she became a recluse. Although that was difficult to do thanks to the lawsuits by those erred by the Card, still in litigation today. About a year after her world crashed, she got herself back up. This would be the last sliver of her life and she was damned if it'd be in mourning. Her husband (not technically her ex-husband but in her eyes, they were) would not cause her any more ruin. And yes, it was a shame that he took her granddaughter with him when he fled, but she couldn't mourn for the child any longer. Her tears dried up, her heart fully black, she found a small house in Greenwich, Connecticut she downgraded to and set her sights on raising money for charities to offset her negligence at Jay's wrongdoings.

"But did you know...?"

That was the scoop all the reporters craved. At first, she bristled. No, she hadn't known. Impossible. But that was a lie. She wasn't a fool. She knew that Jay's business was suspect. Certainly not as suspect as she found it to be, she'd pictured more of the white-collar nature. Not based on hit men and trafficked organs. According to her moral standards, that absolved her of any criminal intent. Before the cameras, she played the role of a naïve woman from a different era. Tried to score some sympathy points. People saw right through. She was an icy witch from WASPy wealthy Connecticut in a burgeoning era where no one could muster sympathy for such a silver spoon. SNL did a skit where she was played by a vampire that sent her into a spiral before she finally let go of what others might think. Let them believe she was a monster, she no longer cared. She'd never turn on the TV or read a newspaper again. She'd start drinking gin by noon and spend days in her tiny garden, pruning. The only line of communication she maintained was with Helene, so she actually wanted to foster that relationship. She and Helene had always been cold toward one another, like mother like daughter. But before she'd be gone from this Earth, that could be the one thing she'd fix.

"Hel," she said, knocking on the door. The doorman had let her up, even though he buzzed Helene's intercom without a reply. Luckily, she had her own set of keys. She struggled with the lock and opened the door to find an unsavory stench. Couldn't Helene light a candle sometime? The windows were stamped closed, the heat blasting even though it wasn't cold outside. She opened them, letting in a New York breeze filled with soot and hamburgers from the restaurant below, but it was an improvement.

She found Helene in bed, which wouldn't have been a surprise except it was four in the afternoon and she could tell this was not a nap.

"Wake up," she said, not one for being gentle. With a push, Helene turned over.

"Go away."

She set out to open to the shades, letting them snap at the top while Helene groaned. Next, she directed her daughter to the shower, stripped her down, kept the water hot, and waited at the door until Helene finished. With a towel tied to her chest, Helene looked lovely. Her gray hair wet and cascading. She was always beautiful, which Vivienne took pride in. Her other son (RIP) had always been tougher to love. Never cute, even as a child. She missed him. She missed her former life.

"Where is Gracie?"

Helene gave a rude shrug.

"When did you last see her?"

Helene gave another shrug. She wandered back into her bedroom and Vivienne followed. She sat by the mirror, brushing the knots from her hair.

"She doesn't want to be around me," Helene said, with another shrug.

Vivienne grabbed the brush from her hands and could have whipped it across her daughter's face.

"I'm not surprised, you're barely upright."

"She gave me some pills."

Vivienne shuddered. She hated drugs of any kind and their sordidness. A martini— the only drug she required.

"She's a dealer, you know that right?" Vivienne

said. "I saw her once in the park, a disheveled man handed her money. I nearly died."

"I can't control her."

Vivienne smacked her across the face. It was easier than continuing this insipid argument. Maybe if she had hit her more often, Helene wouldn't be so weak.

"We're finding her!" Vivienne said, grasping Helene's arm.

"I need to dress!"

"I'm giving you precisely two minutes."

A half hour later, Vivienne and Helene were marching through Central Park on a tear. They held up a picture of Gracie for identification, asking anyone they came into contact with if they had seen this girl. People thought them mad. After an hour of walking around with blisters on their feet, they found a bench. Helene was dressed with her college sweatshirt and some mom jeans, Reeboks. Vivienne didn't know if she was angrier with her daughter's appearance or the whole ludicrous situation.

"She's not the girl who left," Helene said, through tears.

"Is that what you're holding onto?"

"She's cruel and distant."

"Let her be. The things she's seen." Vivienne had never really smoked cigarettes, but she found herself longing for one. "Don't hover over her."

"She's selling drugs."

Vivienne shuddered again. "The most we can hope for is it's a phase."

"How could you allow me to grow up in a house like I did?"

Vivienne pursed her lips. She never enjoyed talking about one's feelings. She found feelings overrated.

"You were given everything—"

"I had a demon for a father."

"Maybe so, but he was never bad to you. He adored you. You were his favorite, over Chip, over even me."

"What does that say about me?"

Vivienne patted her daughter on the shoulder. It was more of a show of affection than she ever gave.

"For all his failings, and he had many..."

Helene gave a side-eye.

"Many, many, but he was a decent father to you. You never wanted for anything."

"How can you not be angrier at him?"

"What would that do? I let go of my resentment. I choose not to really think about him."

"He took my daughter for four years!"

"And what does stewing in that do? There's a benefit to being cold, withdrawn, at a distance. If we never let ourselves get too close, we can never be hurt."

"That's a sad way to live your life."

"Says the woman who wouldn't have gotten out of bed if I hadn't come."

"Mother, what do you want me to do? I'm here now."

"Stop feeling sorry for yourself."

And with that, Vivienne got up and walked away.

Neither of them knew it at the time, but they would never see Gracie again. She vanished into the ether, like she had desired, her final desire. The years crawled by and soon Vivienne passed as well. She had a stroke she never healed from and died in her sleep at a home. Helene was the only one at her funeral. Her son

Brenton was in Europe on a tour at the time and Helene told him not to come home. The coffin lowered, Helene tossed in the dirt, and then went back to bed. It had been a two-year sleep. She'd only fully awaken once she had to identity Gracie's body, after all this time.

**11**

When Gracie left Helene's apartment, she hooked up with a man named Grass. She'd met him in the park and found him inspiring. He seemed to float. No roots, dirt under his fingernails, long hair like a surfer, a grubby sheen to his skin. She pegged him only a few years older and decided he would be the one to show her the world. They had saved up all the money they made from selling drugs to rich idiot kids, purchased a van, and took off.

She wanted as far away from New York City as possible. Its crowds and garbage-lined streets, its moneyed atmosphere. They would forage off the land and wind through every state, then ditch the van in California and head to a place like Fiji. Grass was a musician at heart and she was enamored by his whistling talents. They found a commune somewhere in middle America and she shaved her head and called herself Pearl from *The Scarlet Letter*. Grass and Pearl, they could get you whatever you desired. They just had that spark. She slept under the stars and they found a dog they named Twinkle. They sold herb and a home-made liquor that would make your eyes cross. They made love to the sunrise and she found herself pregnant. She was adamant they name her Desire.

She rarely thought of her mother or brother, but Papa Jay often cluttered her thoughts. She woke up one morning, her belly full with child and wondered if he was still alive. If he had escaped Mexico and the hit on him? If he was still running his business somewhere else?

"Where's your mind, Pearl?" Grass asked, brushing away her hair from her eyes. Grass had a partner who shipped them drugs that they sold around the commune. It allowed them to live there like kings, micro-dosing all they ever wanted.

"It's nowhere," she said, but he could tell she was lying. They were in tune like that. "Sometimes I go back to..."

She'd told him of everything that went down in Mexico. One night on a rooftop in Indiana with two wine coolers between them, she confessed her whole sordid past. He said it only made him love her more.

"...My grandfather," she said, the acid rising in her throat.

He plucked a tiny flower and put it behind his ear. He smelled of lemon and lavender. She nestled into his hairy chest.

"I wonder what happened to him."

"What do you want to happen to him?"

"I don't... I don't know."

It was true. Sometimes she wished him to be tortured, other times freedom.

"How about this?" Grass asked, with a twinkle in

his baby blue eyes. "He led you to me. Had he not taken you, we never would've met."

"That's true."

"Every step you've ever taken led you to my feet. For me to worship your very being."

He held her foot and kissed her toe that had a ring on it.

"Grass?"

"Yes, my dove?"

She grimaced in pain. "I think the baby is coming."

She gave birth by nighttime to Desire, a five pound, three ounces little nugget that she poured all the love she never thought she had into. This would be the moment her life truly shifted, from one of turmoil to one of harmony.

And for a while, it was. She spent the days with Desire attached to her hip. Let Grass take care of the business in the commune while she bonded. Desire was a sweet child. Not prone to crying. A happy, gurgling baby. She found a village at the commune, women who went topless with their own babies on their hips. The commune was built on a giant corn farm, its members drove to Lincoln to sell their wares at the market. The summertime was full of hot sun and bugs, the winter-time snuggly and isolated, but in a good way. Grass read books out loud to her and Desire: Ken Kesey and Thomas Mann, *The Electric Kool-Aid Acid Test* and other titles from the sixties. They were bringing back a long-lost era and she felt sorry for those still in New York surrounded by so much chaos. She was sure her mother had given up the search.

Then came the raid. If one has to ask themselves whether you're in a cult or not, you're in a cult. Deep down, she knew. There was a barn forbidden to her that seemingly held an arsenal of weapons. When the feds closed in one night, she woke up to the smell of smoke. The compound was on fire and screams ushered from windows. Rounds of ammunition went off and it reminded her of the time spent with Papa Jay.

"Damn pigs," Grass said, pulling out a pistol she had no idea he owned.

"What are you doing?"

"Going out in a blaze."

He was high, not an abnormal occurrence, his eyes spinning and bloodshot.

"But Desire," she said, holding out her baby. Desire was crying, a rarity, but who wouldn't cry in a situation like that?

"I gotta protect Tim."

Tim being the supposed "leader," who Grass spoke of with reverential awe. It had never bothered her at first, Tim was good to them. A man with an impressive beard down to his chest and eyes that made it easy to lose yourself. Grass spent a lot of time with Tim and she never suspected an unsavoriness—she was too busy with Desire to notice. But the way Grass spoke of him now—he was in love.

Grass charged outside despite her screams only for the bullets to slice through his body and make him dance in place like a scarecrow in a heavy wind. She had to stop screaming. That would be her and her baby's doom. She grabbed Desire and took off out the back door. Without shoes, the dirt cut into her feet and left a trail of blood. Still, she ran. The compound so big and, in the darkness, hard to tell where she was going. She thought she made it to the thruway but had circled back around by accident to a sea of police sirens. They forced her to put up her hands but she couldn't. She was holding Desire. In the thin sliver of moonlight that cut through the night, she tried to make them see. She pleaded, but they kept repeating for her to raise her arms. And when she wouldn't, they replied with bullets. They ripped through her and Desire. Her last sight of a bloody Desire, falling apart in her hands. She must've gone quickly, Gracie decided. At least, this cruel world would give her that. She sunk to her knees, tears dried to her face, her baby unrecognizable as she let her go to the ground. The police officers closed in. She just wanted it to end. She saw them hovering, the shock on their faces frozen. Let them soak in what they'd done, live with it forever. With blood burbling from her lips, she spat at them.

One last force of life until she choked on her last breath.

## 12

HELENE HAD HEARD ABOUT THE PEOPLE OF THE Sun on the news, but didn't give it a blink. There were a million terrible news stories a day, and this one, while certainly newsworthy, seemed a million miles away in Nebraska. Until some of the names of the dead were released and Gracie Stockton scrolled across the screen. Because of her daughter's earlier notoriety, she was instantly recognized by the FBI. Immediately, Helene booked a flight to Lincoln and flew down.

The coroner's office cold and grim. Gracie's body lay on the slab. Not a peaceful death, this was clear in the shape of Gracie's mouth frozen in a final scream.

"There was a child too, but I don't recommend seeing."

"A child?"

Helene was a grandmother and had no idea. She mourned the loss of this role and had a flash of Gracie around the age of four or five when she first found her love of dance. She twirled through their living room shouting, "I'm a ballerina, I'm a ballerina." Her late husband Harrison was working late and Brenton at soccer camp, so this moment was for Helene alone. Gracie balanced on one toe, which seemed like an impossibility, but Gracie managed to stand strong. And Helene had a vision of her daughter touring the world and sharing her gift with an audience. That was the path she was meant to go on, not this twisted plummet.

The funeral back home was a somber affair. Gracie had no friends anymore and Helene had lost touch with most of her acquaintances from the past. Brenton flew in from Europe where he was living now with a Bulgarian woman. She didn't quite know what he did for a living, something with new-fangled currency and she really didn't care.

"Mom," he said, with a half-hug. He had put on weight, mostly in his face and stomach while she had become frighteningly thin.

The priest spoke over the body, and she tuned it all out. When it was over, she saw a man in the distance wearing sunglasses. He had long, gray hair that curled around his ears.

"Peter?"

"I'll leave you two," Brenton said, and inched away.

Peter had been her lover after her divorce from Harrison and during the early years when Gracie was first taken. He was kind and as patient as can be until she drove him away.

"I'm so sorry," he said, consuming her in a hug. She tightened up, unused to affection but then let herself rest against his pillow-like shoulder. It felt like she must've cried for an hour.

The aftermath of a death was worse than the shock. She wanted to sleep; she wanted to die. She probably would have, if not for Peter. He checked in on her every day. He brought her bagels and lox. They watched the entire *Godfather* series, which she'd never seen before. When she was ready to go outside again, he took her to the Met, MOMA, the Museum of Natural History. He had tickets to Lincoln Center and the Opera. His job was to keep her as busy as possible, to avoid the sinister recesses of her brain.

After six months, she allowed him in her bed. She hadn't been touched since he left her years ago, and she was afraid that the idea of pleasure was something she'd given up. But he was kind and gentle, making sure she was okay the entire time. In the morning, he made her coffee the way she liked it, with all the sugars. He asked if he could move in.

She gave a sad laugh. "Why would you want me?"

"I never stopped loving you."

This sounded greeting-card worthy, but she decided not to judge. The last time she knew happiness, well... She had it with him, for a moment. There was a sweet spot after the divorce from Harrison and before Gracie had been kidnapped where she felt for the first time that she wanted to pause life. But it was fleeting.

"No," she said, and she could see his heart breaking in two. "I mean, yes. But not here."

His eyes perked up.

"Take me away. From everything I know. This city. There's nothing here for me anymore."

He held her hand. "Where do you want to go?"

"This country has done me no favors. I want to go somewhere where I don't have to hear English all the time. Where nothing reminds me of all I lost."

She had lost a lot, more than the average human

should bear. The Card stole her brother Chip years ago, Harrison succumbed to liver disease, her mother from old age, her father vanished, and now Gracie. Brenton was never coming back from Europe. They would check in a few times a year and that would be the extent of their relationship.

"Somewhere far. Unrecognizable," she said.

They settled on Peru. Peter had had business there connected to one of his non-profits and fell in love. She would as well. And she did. They picked Iquitos, which touched the Amazon. She didn't want a place that was too quiet where she'd sink into her thoughts. Iquitos had the vibe of a city, but small enough. They rented an apartment in the middle of the center and she started painting. She had never painted before, but found she was quite good. Enough to sell her pieces at the local fairs and make enough spending money.

Sometimes she would wake up in the middle of the night with the desire to paint. It would call her and she'd be pulled out of bed, in a dream-like state. When this happened, she would leave her body. Where she went, she did not know, but after she'd spiral back, she wouldn't recognize her creation. These paintings were of a tiny hut in the middle of the jungle. She assumed it was the Amazon. In this hut was an old, old woman standing before a fire. The more Helene painted, the more intricate the details. Eventually, she could see that the fire was a body engulfed in flames.

She hid these from Peter; he would think her demonic. For the body in flames was clearly the devil. She knew that in her heart. The other thing she knew was that this hut, those flames, and the old, old woman called to her, her voice like sandpaper. The old woman was close. Just off the jungle, a drive in from Iquitos.

One day, she would take off and go. She knew this so inherently that it chilled her bones. What would be revealed in this hut, this she did not know. But it would change her life. It would settle her. Because she was bullshitting herself here in Peru. She thought she found happiness, but a demon gnawed her from the inside. She would release this demon in the jungle, and then she would return to Peter, fully able to love him whole.

But not yet, this she understood. Only when the time was right. Similar to how she'd be pulled from her bed to paint, the same yearning would take her to this place devoid from Time itself. All the strife in her life would lead her to its door, and she'd be able to breathe again.

This was what kept her going.

What would save her from destruction.

She desired this meeting from the very core of her being.

She simply needed to be patient.

## 13

THE IMAGES ALONG THE CEILING OF THE HUT FADE as William Clark regains his bearings. He'd been so immersed in the vision, he lost sense of his body. No longer trapped by what age had done to it, but now the aches resume. The old woman stands propped up with a walking stick culling the flames in the center. She brings them to a low simmer while her bodyguard still blocks the door. There is no chance of him escaping, not that he wants to. He's curious for her to show him more of what happened to all the people in his life, after the death of his wife Vivienne, not a surprise, and Gracie's, although he thought the child would've been tenacious enough to survive anything.

"What do you have to say?" the old woman asks. She's chewing on seeds that get stuck between her teeth. They are bright red and look like tiny squished ants.

"You want me to feel bad?"

"I do not want anything from you."

She eyes her bodyguard who grimaces. He hadn't

fully looked at the bodyguard before, but there's a resemblance that's uncanny. The man looks like he did over forty years ago when William Clark was pushing middle age.

"Is that supposed to be me?"

The old woman spits the seeds at the fire that grows in height.

"It is not you, that I can assure you."

"What is the purpose of all of this?"

The old woman fixes her cloak that has begun to sag. She seems familiar as well, but he's met so many people over the course of his life, it's hard to pinpoint how he knows her. But he does. Much like everyone she'd shown has been affected by an association to him, he's certain he did her wrong. This is her form of revenge.

"How did it feel to learn the fate of your grand-daughter?"

"I do not believe in emotions."

"Your wife said the same thing."

"Yes, it was a commonality we shared."

"Do you mourn her death?"

"Vivienne? No. She and I always had a rather busi-ness-like relationship."

"And Gracie?"

"Am I in mourning over her death...no. Do I wish it didn't happen...yes."

"So, you can show emotion?"

"No, I can have an opinion."

She spits another seed into the fire that rages.

"Is that what this is about?" he asks. "Seeing if I have emotions?"

The old woman shakes her head. "This is not *about* anything. It just is."

"Nothing just is. Everything has a purpose. Everyone has a design, a goal. You want something from me."

"I am merely a conduit."

"To?"

She looks up through the hole in the ceiling of the hut to the black sky dotted with stars.

"The universe."

"Okay, you are a conduit to the universe, that is what you are saying?"

"That is what you inferred."

"Why be so cryptic?"

She spits another seed. In the flames, a vision of a baby boy appears. "Do you see this?"

"A baby?"

"Yes, not just any baby. You."

"That is me?"

She gives a firm nod. "If I am searching for anything, it is answers."

"Okay, I'll play along. What is of interest?"

"The very notion of evil. Where it stems."

"You think I'm evil?"

"This is a certainty."

"Evil is subjective."

"Only someone with evil in their heart would say that."

"All right, you seem to know everything about me. You've known what I've done. You deemed me ev..." He begins choking, dredging up a ball of phlegm that's ringed with blood. "What more is there to figure out?"

"Have you always been a being of evil, or did it enter you? Were you simply unlucky?"

"You mean, have I been possessed?"

"This is what the universe questions."

"And who in the universe has questioned?"

She smiles a red-tooth smile. "Again, I am a conduit. This I do not know."

"Yes, I've had people killed. Many have died at my hands. So, you are saying that is due to a possession? When I was a child?"

"You have no feelings hearing your granddaughter and great-granddaughter suffered a brutal death."

"I told you I do not feel emotions. Never had. I think the proper term is a sociopath. But how can one be labeled evil for innately who they are?"

"This is the crux of what we are trying to decipher."

"Okay. I understand your purpose. You are a detective of sorts. I've been called here for you to decide whether I was born evil, or if I picked it up along the way."

"What do you think it is?"

"Again, I don't believe I'm evil. I am self-serving."

"You daughter Helene...?"

"What about her?"

"Of everyone in your life, you care for her the most. Doesn't it bother you that she hates you so?"

"I would hate me too. I took away her daughter."

"But you don't feel bad?"

"Again. That is an emotion."

"I do not believe that you don't feel anything. Your business...the Card, it brings you satisfaction?"

"Of course."

"Is that why you created the organization?"

He stares into the old woman eyes and has a flicker of remembrance. This was someone he'd been intimate with, a very long time ago. From the way she speaks, with such hatred in her voice, there was once a passion between them.

"We knew each other, yes?"

She chews on her tongue.

"You loved me once. If I could just see your face..."

He reaches out to part the hair that covers her. There's something in her smile that takes him back, the sadness it evokes. But the force of the flame erupts between them, creating a wall. The bodyguard reacts by pulling him away. He wrestles in this man's arms, but he's too old and puny to fight.

"You will keep your distance," the bodyguard says, twisting his arm.

"Yes, yes, I understand."

The flames calm down, the old woman slightly ruffled. He got under her skin a little, which means he can do it again.

"I did you wrong," he says.

"Everyone you've been in contact with you've done wrong."

"So, you are not disagreeing?"

She glances the other way, her mouth trembling. Looks up to the sky, as if to quell a source of energy. She breathes in the air until she's full again.

"If I did you wrong, is it an apology you want?"

At this, she laughs, a cruel treble. "No. No, no, no. I have no need for that."

"But I did do you wrong?"

"Gable," she says, quietly, and then clamps her mouth shut.

"Ah, yes, that is how you knew me. I am Gable to you."

"You are *nothing* to me, let us get that clear."

"Fine, but in another life when we knew one another, I was Gable. I wore a mask."

"You always wear a mask."

"But a specific mask, yes? That of a screen legend. That of my other persona."

He scans his mind as to who she could be. A list of employees, but he can barely recall any who survived.

"You are trying to think of who I am?"

"If I could know, then I can properly make amends."

"Let me let you in on a little secret. There is nothing you can do or say that will lead you out of this hut. You are already dead."

"So, I'm between two worlds, is that what this is? I have died and I am being judged about where I am sent to next?"

"What I mean is that your death is inevitable. Once you entered this hut, you already died for there is no chance of you leaving."

"You will kill me?"

"That is the only guarantee I can offer. So, you might as well make the most of this short time you have left. I have showed you two visions of those whose lives you altered and you were barely affected. I strongly urge you to look deeper during the next one. Leave this Earth receiving this gift I am giving you. One of understanding as to why you do the things you do."

"Who is next on this strange trip?"

"You have seen how your family has suffered, but

what of your other family, that of the Card and those who gave you their lives?"

"A former operative?"

"Not many have survived. Can you think of any?"

"Yes. Of course. The one who I was never able to ice."

And then, at the same time, they both say: "JD Storm."

## 14

FOR THE PAST FEW YEARS, JD STORM'S MISSION HAS not changed: find Gable, a.k.a. Jay Howell, a.k.a. whatever alias he was using now. The only difference from the past was that Gable was no longer looking for him. After JD left the Card, a sin that no other departed operative ever lived to tell, he became a hunted man on the run. He kidnapped Gable's daughter, just to give himself leverage. If it came to it, he'd give her back in exchange for his final freedom. But all things related to the Card never go smoothly.

It was when Gable killed his old girlfriend Annie that really set him on this path of revenge. The hardest part being that he never found out if she'd been working with Gable all along to sell him out. Maybe it was best he never learned and could keep her sainted in his mind. One would think in this day and age that locating a person shouldn't be too hard. People leave trails behind. But not Gable. He'd spent his whole life preparing for the chance that he might need to disappear. And disappear he did.

To make ends meet, JD picked up some odd jobs. He was never one to set down roots, so he flitted across the country. Construction jobs, security, bouncer, anything that paid under the table. The search for Gable became a goalpost, but he knew there'd be a slim chance in finding the man. Especially in the parts of the country he frequented. Gable was likely internationally based in a place where no one would recognize his face. If he even kept his same face. The Card was all about changing one's façade. He'd bet that Gable long shed his.

He was working security detail in Maryland, shadowing a guy who needed to be shadowed (that was all the info given to him). The guy would call and JD would drive him around to meetings that usually took place outside on the waterfront. JD saw cash handed back and forth through the rearview, but it wasn't in his job description to ask. One time, whoever the guy handed cash to wasn't happy with the amount and fists began to fly. JD shot out of the SUV, ran over with an elbow to the throat. The other guy dropped to his knees, hacking. Then they pushed him into the waters, got back in the car and drove away.

"That was some quick moves," the guy said. "I appreciate."

"You hired me."

The guy squinted his eyes, gave JD a good look over. People did this to him often on account of his missing eye. He used to have a glass one but it shattered.

"Soldier, right?"

This was true. Fought in Iraq, saw some unfathomable shit. It all paled in comparison to the hell he entered after. He thought he experienced the worst of humanity in war, turns out it'd be at the Card.

"You don't have to say," the guy said, throwing up his hands. "You just have that look to ya. If there's anything I could ever do...to thank you? That asshole was packing, so it coulda ended up way different. Alls I'm saying is, if you ever needed a favor?"

JD eyed him with his good eye through the rearview. "I need someone found."

"Found, eh? Like killed?"

"I want to be the one to do it."

JD gave him all the details and the guy said he'd try. He knew another guy who worked as a PI. JD assured him that Gable wasn't in the States, and the guy suggested Mexico.

"He wouldn't have wanted to get on any airplanes, so it's Mexico or Canada."

"He had business in Mexico."

"Then that's where he fled."

"I've been down there," JD said. All the money he made from his odd jobs went to a trip down south. He spanned the country with Gable's picture for about two months, slept on the beach, showered in the ocean. He came home wishing he enjoyed the paradise, not been so laser focused. Although had he not, he'd be kicking himself for not trying harder.

He stayed working for this guy, got a tiny apartment by the water. The fact that someone else had taken the reins in finding Gable allowed him to relax. The guy paid really well, he was definitely mobbed up, but JD didn't care. This guy was a boss unlike Gable. He invited JD over to his family's house. His wife made him Sunday fish. The PI kept hunting for Gable without any leads and eventually JD no longer thought about revenge every day. For years Gable had been such a parasitical part of his life, he hadn't even realized how much he'd been obsessed. He always figured himself a logical person, but trauma had fucked with his head. It took him out of his body, made him weak. So what if he never found Gable? Annie was still dead. There was nothing that could be done. It was the unfairness that nagged at him. That the universe would be content with letting a monster go free. He always believed there had to be a balance. That no one person could be so evil. It was time to accept that when it comes to the universe, there are no absolutes.

But then, a nugget. The PI came across the newspaper headline about Gracie Stockton returning home. Her grandfather had kidnapped her to Mexico after all, which made JD at least feel that he'd probably been close. There'd been a shootout at Gable's headquarters, then he fled. Again, he could be anywhere. But a fire stoked, a tickle in his belly. Gable left people behind in Mexico who might have an inkling as to where he went. This would be the last time he'd hunt the man. If he came up fruitless, he'd let Gable go. But he had to try.

So, he called Bonner.

15

MONICA BONNER USED TO IDENTIFY HERSELF BY labels: Detective, Mother, Wife. She was no longer any of those. They existed from a part of her life so long ago, the memories were becoming hard to access. When her child Kellan died, her marriage fell apart and two of those roles dissolved. Then when she failed to get Gracie Stockton back to her family, she didn't have the drive for police work anymore. She'd moved aside one obsession: that of the death of her son and traded it for another. Whatever it took, she'd locate Gracie's grandfather and finally bring the child home. Not being constricted by police procedure would actually help bring justice forth. She'd seen it many times before.

But there is only so much failure one person can take. The wall of pictures that used to hold Kellan became replaced with tracking Jay Howell down. If one were to enter her house, they would think her mad. Newspaper articles spanned the entire length of her apartment held up by push-pins. Scribbles with a red pen marked any glimmer as to his whereabouts. But these searches were fruitless. Every time she thought she unlocked the mystery to his location, it sent her down a dead-end trail. So much so, that she'd wrung her hands and given up.

There had been bouts to Canada and Mexico, assuming he had left the States. Even though Jay Howell's money had been cut-off, he had to have offshore accounts that the FBI couldn't trace. Enough to get him on a private jet somewhere, anywhere. Since she left her job, her bank account was slim. There'd be no way she could travel across the globe in pursuit. So, slowly she began to take her findings down from the wall. She replaced it with a reprinted Jackson Pollock painting that allowed her to lose all her thoughts when she stared at its colorful swirls. She had stopped being a police officer years ago, but hadn't really stopped until that painting went up.

There had been a trip down to Mexico once. She floated from town to town because her money went far. There wasn't as much of a rush, since motels came cheap. She was in a town she couldn't remember the name of when she came across a man she recognized. He had one eye, the other as if the eyeball had been scooped out. Back when she located Jay Howell's safe house, she pursued without the FBI as back up. Jay Howell had shot a man who was bleeding on the ground before he took off. Monica made sure he kept pressure on the wound to staunch the flow. He was unmemorable, especially because of the intensity of the situation where she feared she might not make it out alive, but she remembered his missing eye. That wasn't something one forgot.

She'd been wandering an empty beach around

dusk. Just figuring out her life and what her next step would be. This trip to Mexico would likely be the last time she went all out to find Jay Howell. She lacked the energy to fight any more, but contemplated her second act. She was forty years old, young enough to start again. She'd spent the last few years in New York City, but it wasn't really for her. Too crowded, too noisy, too impersonal. And a small town would be too quiet, people too nosy. She needed to find a place where she could breathe but also keep her mind active. The answer may lie outside of the States in a place where she knew no one.

She'd been observing the tides washing away seashells when a man was walking her way. He was well-built, not a native, his pale skin fried and reddened by the unrelenting sun. He moved with a purpose she found suspect. Even though she was no longer a detective, that instinct remained. This was a man who had secrets and moved in the shadows. This thrilled her.

As they approached, she offered a smile. Nothing too overt, just one to capture his interest. She noticed his missing eye and had a flash of when she'd seen it last. Similarly, this man gave a hint of recognition too. She imagined he wasn't the type to be spooked, but he was rattled then. It was as if he started to smile and then realized the implications. He quickly back-peddled and took off along the shoreline.

Now, Monica may have left the force, but she still kept fit. Her work-outs became her meditation and although she didn't have a huge physical presence, she was squat and muscular. She took off after him, catching up quickly.

"Wait, wait," she called out, tackling him to the

sand. They rolled around like lovers, sand in their eyes. "I know you."

"You don't," he said, a weak response.

She pinned him down. He was strong enough to push her off of him, but he didn't, which made her realize he was kind. She'd been getting into energies and could feel his. He exuded a positive aura, not perfect, but good enough to trust.

"You were at the safe house," she said. "The girl...Gracie."

He blinked his good eye, as if to say, yes.

They found a bar at the end of the beach that served *cerveza*. The sun was setting and they looked like two honeymooners to the locals. The radio played a song that made her sway. She sucked on a lime and took a sip of the beer that was cold. Neither of them spoke for minute, taking in the situation, sizing each other up.

"Bonner," she finally said, holding out a hand. "Monica Bonner."

"The detective?"

She shook her head. "Not anymore. Regular civilian here now."

"JD," he said, into his beer. "Storm."

"JD Storm, that's a name."

"I've had others, but this is the one that has stuck the most."

She didn't know what to say to that. JD wasn't a man that spoke much, his world internal. His hair had gotten longer since she saw him last, down to his shoulders now, flicked with gray.

"What are you in Mexico for?" she asked.

He clenched his hands. "I believe I'm looking for the same man as you."

They traded war stories of the last few years, astonished at how closely their paths aligned many times. How the thrust of their lives had been this one, elusive man. How each time they returned empty-handed; it stole a bit of their soul. How both were ready to give up.

"It became about the chase, no longer the girl," she said, on her second beer now. She let her hair out of a ponytail, shook it in the wind. She was feeling flirty in a way she hadn't felt since before her marriage. She wanted this man, this hulking stranger. She desired him to take her away from the present moment, spend a night together where she'd forget who she was and why she still woke up crying every morning. Pressed underneath his body, she wouldn't be the woman who lost her son to cancer, whose life was a series of unending disappointments.

"I get that," he said, signaling the bartender for another one. When he arrived, he popped it open against the wooden bar and sucked down half. "A purpose, but..." He stopped, chewed his lip. "That's no purpose, it's a way of preventing moving forward."

She gulped, as if he'd relayed her deepest secrets.

"I want to move forward, but..."

She told him about Kellan, how his death tore her in two. It used to be that Kellan visited her all the time: in thoughts, in dreams. Now, years later, she was losing him. He felt so far away that she couldn't reach him anymore. She never laundered his clothes and they held his smell but now even that had faded. There was nothing left of him at all.

"Gable killed my girlfriend," JD said. "My ex...well, it's complicated. So it became an eye for an eye situation."

This embarrassed her. "Oh."

But he smiled. "I didn't realize the joke." He pointed at the gaping hole where his eye used to be. "A souvenir from Iraq. Used to wear a patch, but I don't give a fuck anymore. Let people stare. This is me."

She found herself staring at his empty socket the same way she'd observe her Jackson Pollock painting. For a moment, she lost herself in its pull as if he held the mysteries of the universe in his non-gaze. When she came to, she had to apologize.

"I wasn't staring."

"You were."

"Not in the way you think. There's something calming about... I'm sorry, that's so rude of me, talking about your injury."

"Most shy away from it."

"Scars tell our stories." She had heard that in some movie and felt dumb for repeating it, but it actually was true. She pulled up her shirt, showing a nasty scar below her left breast. "Perp sliced me good. Just a routine breaking and entering but he got scared. Hurt like hell."

JD nodded; he had many too.

They traded their war stories, becoming intimate in a way that most never do—those who've led rather untouched lives. She fingered one of his scars, a diagonal one down his thigh. He shivered when she touched it.

The sun had almost set, a tiny orange ball licking the horizon. A spew of reds and purples shot out across the sky. She still had her hand on his thigh. The bartender was washing a glass with a rag, whistling through his mustache.

"You? Room?" the bartender asked in his staccato English. He pointed his thumb at a tiny house next to a slightly bigger one.

By the time they made their way, night had arrived. The air was crisp, redolent with the salt of the water. The entire house was one room with a twin bed in the corner. She hadn't been with anyone since her ex-husband years ago and could feel the same hesitation in him. Both had journeyed solo for so long. He pressed on top of her and she found herself saying, "Squeeze me hard, so hard I can't feel anything else."

"I don't want to hurt you, Bonner."

"You won't. I can't. I want to feel."

Her squeezed her tight and they made love to the crashing waves. They explored each other's bodies all night, untamed. She longed to be devoured, to exist inside of him. She'd never had these feelings before with her ex. With JD on top, his one eye locked on hers, she was safe. The world was not the scary place that had almost destroyed her. There were pockets where she could be alive again, find the girl she had lost.

They spent the next few days together, existing in lust, barely words shared between them. Both feared that conversation would shatter this bubble. And neither needed words at that moment, only carnal desires. When they couldn't fuck anymore, they were forced to speak and found that neither really had anything to say. Strip away the similarities that brought them to this beach in Mexico, the obsessions that consumed them, and they had little in common. They could try to search for Jay Howell more, but she could tell JD was far away now.

"You don't have to stay," she said, their third night

together. The twin bed was becoming increasingly hard to sleep in together, and he'd taken to the floor with only a pillow.

"I'm not good at...this."

"What is this?"

"I don't know."

"I'm not good at it either. So, we have that at least."

"I'm used to...well, being alone, not having anyone to rely on. It's always been that way. Folks died early on, raised by my Gramps who then died too. Went into the military soon after."

"The girl you spoke of, your ex..."

She instantly regretted it. Jay Howell had killed his former love and she was cruel for bringing her up in any way.

"I was more open then. It was before Iraq, before the Card. I was a different person."

"I understand."

"I mean, I'm not great at conversation. Having to talk all the time. Sometimes I go days without speaking to someone. I like my solitude."

"Do you?"

"I do. I'm used to it. It's how I'm comfortable."

Solitude had been all she knew for some time. The thought of having a family again was like an electric zap, equally thrilling and painful.

"I don't know if I want to be comfortable anymore," she said with the kind of sigh that could make someone cry if they heard.

"This was really special. I mean it. Unexpected. But you'll grow tired of me. I don't offer enough."

"That you can say that about yourself–"

"It's how I choose to exist. I'm half a man, and I'm

content with this. Really, I am. If I let someone get close…that's how I lose them. Because I'm nuclear."

She placed her hand on his heart. "I'd like to try to get to know you."

He didn't answer right away, let her squirm. She hated him for this. Deep down, she didn't want him like that. A boyfriend? A husband down the line? She was asking for a difficult life with someone like him. Could two sad people ever be truly happy together? Or would the sadness just grow and grow before it spread like a cancer? She thought of her son, felt a tear welling.

He took her hand off his heart. "Maybe someday, but not today. I should go."

It was the middle of the night, the beach encased in pure darkness. Even the moon wasn't out. Where would he go? But she remembered how she perceived him when they first crossed paths on the shore. He was someone who flitted in the shadows. He would find his way.

"Can I give you my number?" she asked.

"I don't have a phone."

"For you to have. You don't need a phone. There are phones everywhere."

"You're aware I might never call?"

"That's fine, but this way if we ever get a lead on Jay Howell…"

She found a pen and tore out a page from the Bible in a drawer, scribbled her number.

"You're upset?" he asked.

"No, no I'm not. This was a fantasy and it was time for it to end. I'm aware we're not right for each other."

"It's that you deserve more."

"I get it, you're self-deprecating."

"Will you be okay? Getting back home, or will you stay in Mexico?"

She hadn't thought about it, almost forgetting where they were. Her life had been this tiny house for the last few days.

"I'll be fine," she said, and truly meant it. Now that she said it, she wanted him to go. All of his idiosyncrasies became heightened: the sleeping on the floor bit, how she was always the one to initiate anything sexual, the way everything he did was with military precision from the way he walked, to the way he talked, and the fact she had no idea who this man was besides his name (which could be a lie) and the few terrible traumas from his life that he peppered their conversations with. One night she woke up while he writhed on the floor as if he was wrestling a bear. She could tell in this phantom fight that he won.

He stood there and she wondered if he was going to kiss her. They had fucked every which way, but hadn't kissed. That should've been red flag number one. But then he moved in for one, his thin lips parting. She wouldn't give him hers. She turned away, only allowed her cheek. He was startled at first, but planted a peck that one would give to their aunt. Then he was out the door.

She watched him, a dark figure swallowed up by even more darkness, pushing his way across the sand. She couldn't tell if she could see him anymore, but wasn't ready to shut the door. To close the door meant an end to this entire tryst and she had goosebumps wondering if she ever might be thrilled like this again.

But it was a long life and she had lived many lives already. She could and would open herself up again.

She'd leave Mexico and find a new purpose, one that took away the sadness.

She shut the door against a heavy gust of wind.

Put him out of her mind for an entire year until her phone rang one day and the gruff voice on the other end said, "Bonner."

16

"Bonner?"

He had no idea how she'd respond. If she'd hang up, curse him out. They'd spent three days on a beach in Mexico making love, then he up and left. But she had given him her number. She said if he ever had a lead on Gable to contact her.

"Yes?"

No one had called her Bonner in a long time. It could either be her old partner Ramirez, who had moved down to Miami, or...

"JD?"

"The one and only."

He laughed, his sense of humor coming back after all this time.

"What do you want?" she asked. She wouldn't play nice. After he left her in Mexico, she roamed around, aimless. She had no drive to find Jay Howell, no pull to do anything but drink tequila and watch the waves. She stayed in that little house on the shore until the rainy season washed her out. Back in the States, she moved in with her mother. Not the best choice, but she was afraid of being alone. Her mother cloying, but sweet. She catered to Monica. Had moved down to St. Pete to be a winter bird. They had a two-room apartment and Monica got a job waitressing. It was a friend of her mother who owned the place. A seafood shack that fried fish well. The job proved a distraction. She met a man named Casey who had a boat. He was older than her by a decade and doted on her. After work, they'd take his boat out, drink beers on the water. She soon started to look sun-kissed. He asked her to move in with him and her mother nudged her to do so. Said she wasn't getting younger and when opportunity knocked... Monica was considering it when the phone rang and JD's voice popped up on the other end.

"The girl is back home," was all he said.

She gripped the phone, shooed her cat away from the table where she was eating from a bowl of grapes. "Which girl? What?"

"*The* girl, Gracie Stockton."

"Wait, they found Jay Howell?"

"Negative. She escaped from his place in Mexico, found her way back to the States. She's not giving interviews, so that's a dead end, but we have a location of where he was keeping her. He's obviously long gone, but someone close by must know something."

There was an excitement to his voice. She couldn't remember him ever sounding that way. This was a different JD, and she didn't know if that pleased her. A headache was forming.

"JD... I-I'm no longer in the chasing game."

"Come now. You're a hunter. Once a hunter, always—"

"No, I'm living in Florida. I got a job."

*I got a man*, she wanted to say too.

He wondered if she'd met someone. Didn't blame her. It'd be foolish to think she would ever wait for him. But he'd thought about her a lot over these past years. He had some flings since, scratched his itch, but he couldn't recall any of those women, only Bonner. Wishing he never left her because he'd gotten scared at getting close.

"Tell your job you need a couple of days," he said. "We'll travel down and just ask around. This is an opportunity that will be gone if we don't make use of it."

She wanted to yell at him to leave her alone. Slam the phone down, except for the fact that cell phones were tough to hang up that way, but he needed to understand that she didn't appreciate him contacting her after all this time. They had fucked years ago, big deal. Both of them used Jay Howell as a way of avoiding the void in their own lives. That didn't give him the right to bother her like this, to get these emotions stewing again.

He was getting nervous that she hadn't responded and wondered if he sold this in the right way. If he should've asked about her life first, caught up before revealing this bombshell. She likely thought him psychotic, the same as most people he encountered.

"JD?" she said, picturing herself on a boat with her current beau. But while he was decent to her, their relationship lacked a spark. They only had sex when planned and he was too old to have kids again, since his now had kids of their own. Why was she staying with him besides the fear of being alone? It was why she fled to her mother's. She was in hiding and if she stayed here, she'd wake up one day an old woman who hadn't really done much of anything with her life for the last few decades.

"I'm in," she said, with a gulp.

They met in the airport in Mexico City the next day, giving an awkward hug by the baggage pick-up. He looked less built than he had when they'd been intimate. Still imposing but with a hard middle-aged gut that most men his age get. She stopped dying her hair so much, let it go gray in fits and spurts. The Florida sun brought out her freckles and she was dressed in jeans shorts and sandals, seashells around her neck, bracelets on her arm. He wore the most nondescript outfit he could find: khaki pants and a black shirt that hugged his biceps.

"I rented a car," he said, and she followed him to a used Volvo that puttered along back-roads until they reached the town where Gable had fled all these years.

It was the rainy season, the same time of year when Monica was there last. The roads slick with mud, the sky opening up at whim. It was a five-hour drive and they did most of it in silence. She realized that he was someone she could be silent with and not feel the need to talk. And how that was a connection she longed to have.

Around hour four, he spoke: "Your job give you trouble with leaving?"

"No." She laughed. "They fired me."

"Oh. Well. Sorry."

"I slung fish at a poorly-attended restaurant. I never should've taken it in the first place."

"It's an honest work," he said, which led her to believe that his current line of work was not so honest.

"I left my guy too," she said.

His ears perked up at this and he tried to hide a smile. "Oh, I didn't know you were seeing someone?"

"Yeah, I was... But it wasn't right in a lot of ways. He didn't..."

She wanted to say *light my fire*.

"Light your fire?" he asked, and her mouth dropped. He had a smirk to him that she found delicious. She barely remembered him smiling when they were together.

"You seem different, JD. More...at ease."

"Yeah, I guess I am. I found a decent job, got a place I've been at in Maryland for a while. I kinda left the old JD behind, ya-know? He creeps back now and again, but I've got him in control. This new JD is a clean slate."

She fiddled with the radio. "I should take notes."

"You seem like you started a new life."

"Nah, more like biding time. Waiting for... I don't know what I'm waiting for."

"Me to call?"

She cut him a look.

He threw up his hands. "Sorry, sorry, I was really an asshole to leave you like I did. You...I liked you. I did. And that scared me if I'm being honest."

"It was scaring me a little too."

"Anyway, we would've been a disaster had I stayed. I had another year or so of abusing myself till I let that go. I found ways of looking within better. Just being kind to myself."

"Yeah, that's important. I'm the worst. I used to

blame myself for Kellan—my son's—death. I know I wasn't responsible but I brought him into the world just to live such a short time. Was it worth it?"

"You can't go there."

"No, I know. I don't anymore. I know I did everything I could to keep him alive—me and Jim. He was a good father. We were a good family when things were working out."

They were the only car on the road, feeling like they were the only two people in existence. The rain slapping against their roof, blurring it all.

"What do we do when we get there?" she asked.

He scratched his chin. "We start at their safe house and just start asking around. I got some money and we can pay anyone off."

"And if we get a clue?"

"We chase it, right?"

"And if we find him?"

He stuck his tongue into his cheek. His good eye glancing in her direction. "We burn him to the fucking ground."

**17**

THEY SPENT A WEEK ASKING AROUND AND BURNING holes through their pockets as their money dried up. All anyone had to offer were the same snippets from the news outlets about the services Gable, or William Clark as he was known here, provided if you needed young girls on the sly or a bevy of drugs. As for Gracie, she was well known in town and they were told she liked to dance. At first, both of them thought the worst that she might've been stripping, but they were pointed to a ballet dance studio owned by a woman named Valeria. For years, a giant black SUV pulled up in front of the studio and Gracie would be led inside by a bodyguard. They were told that this bodyguard had been killed along with all of William Clark's other associates. And said he fled somewhere on a boat. This meant they knew he hadn't gotten on a plane, at least from Mexico. He could be further south, or in Central or South America. That was a lot more than they had before they started asking.

They went to Valeria's studio right away. The

woman was teaching a class with young girls, so they waited until she finished and all the parents had come to pick up their children. They told her they were thinking of signing up their daughter. When Valeria asked her name, they replied, "Gracie."

Valeria showed her fangs. She looked like she wanted to rip off their heads. No one else was in the studio and her fear was apparent by the beads of sweat on her upper lip. She removed a tiny knife kept in a sling attached to her leg.

"What do you want?"

They raised their hands.

"Nothing, *Señora*," JD said. "Only a few questions, then we'll be out of your way."

"Who sent you?"

She was almost crying; they had scared her so.

"We're looking for him," Monica said. "We just want a clue as to where he may have gone?"

"I do not know this."

Valeria's eyes flitted from side to side, scoping out the room, gaging if they were followed.

"I had her taken to the airport," she said, swallowing hard.

Monica nodded. "That was very kind of you."

"They killed my nephew, her bodyguard."

"Who did?"

"Whoever his enemy was."

JD stepped closer. "We heard the man we're after got on a boat."

She still held the knife, waved it around.

"Of course he did, how else would he leave?"

JD took another step and swiped the knife from her hand. She let out a cry as she collapsed to the floor.

"Please leave me. They watch. I know they do. I am forever in danger."

"We don't want to hurt you," Monica said.

"Why are you here?" Valeria shouted, squeezing her fists.

"He took..." Monica began to say, but then realized her answer was meaningless. William Clark took Gracie, but Gracie was home. What more did they really need from him? To see him tortured? Would that be enough?

"He is a menace to this world," JD thundered. "He will destroy again and again unless he is destroyed. He leaves behind a path of flames and therefore needs to be incinerated."

"May I...?" Valeria asked, pulling out a cigarette case, and then lit one when they nodded. "I understand this. I have wanted this man's death too for what he has done. But I am convinced of something. He is not of this world, completely, no man like him is. And therefore, you can not kill him."

She blew a line a smoke that danced with the dust in the room.

JD grimaced. "We *will*."

"I am not saying he will not be killed," Valeria continued. "I am saying the two of you will not be the one to fully kill him. You need someone more in tune..."

"In tune with what?" Monica asked.

"The push and pull of the universe. Someone able to balance out his evil. That is the only way to bring all of him down."

"What kind of person is this?"

"Not a person, no. A being. A shaman."

A crack of lightning flashed outside the windows as a clap of thunder shook their bones.

"A shaman?" JD asked. "What the fuck does that even mean?"

Valeria scrunched up her nose. "Down in Mexico, through Central America, South America are many, many shaman. They are healers, but that is a broad definition of the word. For to heal would be to kill him, yes? Better for the world. So that is who you must find."

"A shaman to kill Gable," Monica repeated.

"Not just any shaman, the right one. The one destined to be his undoing."

"And how do we find this shaman?" Monica asked, but Valeria simply shrugged.

"I am offering advice, not answers. Do either of you need to go back home right now?"

JD and Monica looked at one another and shrugged as well.

"Then time is not important. Wind your way down through these lands, inquire of a shaman that is best at tampering evil. Use them to locate the evil they seek. Evil leaves a trail, a nasty scent. They will be able to pick it up. You have nothing to lose. May I have my knife back?"

JD handed it over.

"Thank you. Now leave me alone. You have caught me in a moment where no one is guarding me. I will not make that same mistake again. I will kill you if you come back because I have nothing to lose either."

Valeria placed her knife back in its slip and walked off. When they left, it was raining even harder, loud drumbeats against the earth. But a seed had been planted inside of them. It was being watered, nurtured, and it would grow. They would leave Mexico because William Clark had clearly left it too. They would find this shaman that would bring forth his end. They didn't have to say it to one another, but committed to this prophecy and would die rather than not see it through.

DESIRE AND... 85

18

THE HUNT FOR A SHAMAN BECAME A YEARS LONG affair for JD and Monica. They wound down the Southern coast of Mexico seeking a connection that they couldn't quite put into words. They drank *ayahuasca*, had good and bad trips, took off down through Central America and came across a shaman who called himself O. O was a short man with a very long ponytail, the sides of his head shaved like in the military. He had a fatherly face, which was how Monica described him. They were wandering in El Petén, pitching a tent they carried around, living lean. They ate what they foraged, making sure that nothing was poisonous. They slept under the stars. This was their second year of journeying and both felt like they knew the other well. JD always cool and calm, an offset to Monica's anxiety. She began to ease as they traveled further away from their old lives. And he opened up more. Not only his past but his present thoughts and feelings. He was a complex man and she wanted to crack every bit of him.

They were greeted one morning by a rising yellow sun and O leaning against a nearby tree. He smoked a *mapacho* cigar down to the nub. He told them with his eyes who he was. They found themselves leaving their tent and following him to a hut where a small fire licked and a woman stirred from a bucket.

*Come*, O said with his eyes. He was mute and they understood this. They sat on logs as the woman filled two wooden cups with her creation. It smelled like bog water and tasted not much better, but they gulped it down as their pupils got big. With his *mapacho* cigar lit, the flaming cherry held their gaze. Because O was mute, the woman sang the *icaros*, a repetitive chant that warmed their bodies. She had a voice that seemed to melt, echoing throughout the jungle. They could hear animals being called, scampering up to the hut, listening in awe.

O entered their minds. *I am O*, he said. *And you will be open. To be open is to unlock your mind, your heart, your soul. You have come for a singular purpose, but there are other purposes that must be crossed off first. You both hold pain. I want you to release that pain. This pain has weighed you down for too long. You may think you have gotten to the other side of it, but that is that how pain works. It is sneaky. It will attack you again and again for the rest of your lives. It will bleed into your next lives and the lives of your offspring. We carry around millennia's worth of trauma, but I will take that pain for you. I will blow smoke at it and send it to the sky. But you have to let me in.*

They agreed.

The woman's voice became louder, eclipsing the entire hut, the entire world, as they dove within. A shooting of diamonds appeared across their vision. The hut melted and oozed. They traveled out of this sphere to another plane. For JD, he was back in Iraq holding a bleeding baby dead in his arms. For Monica, she was holding the hand of her son Kellan on his deathbed. Both the baby and Kellan told each to let them go. JD was responsible for this murder. As a sniper, sometimes there were innocent casualties, this baby being one of them. This life that was just started and cruelly taken away all because of his trigger finger. The baby told him that it didn't blame him anymore. In war, no one is innocent, no one guilty. It is humankind at their worst. The war being bigger than JD himself; he was only a pawn. He needed to forgive himself. He needed to love himself again. JD placed the baby back on the ground and it walked away with half its face shot off. To let this baby go meant that it could finally be free. It no longer wanted to be tethered to him, two strangers bound by unfortunate circumstance. The baby walked away into the desert, blending into the swirls of sand. JD would not visit Iraq again in his mind, the memory nothing more than a mirage.

For Monica, it was harder to let go. The very thing causing her pain being the one person she had loved most in this world. Kellan was her soulmate, she truly believed. The roles should've been reversed where he'd be holding her hand on her deathbed forty years into the future. To actually feel his life slip away. To see him blink for the last time, his eyes clouded with death, clawing with his other hand and trying to grasp onto her. He was not ready to leave, but he was ready to release his pain. And then after he died, they put a sheet over his tiny body grown so small from all the weight he lost. She tried to search for his presence in the air, but couldn't feel him, couldn't smell him anymore. This was the moment she'd replay again and again. The one that invaded her dreams. The knife in her soul. She hadn't been living for too long. She'd taken down all his pictures but still tortured herself that she couldn't protect him from inevitability. That was what parents were supposed to do—protect their child and she failed.

*No, you did not,* O said, as she followed the cherry of his cigar through the darkness. *You did everything in your power to give him as much love as possible during his end. And he still exists. His energy is in your memory. Do not forget him, the good times. But leave behind the tragedy. He is more than the son who got sick. That is not what made him special. You have access to all the wonderful memories you shared. Those are what you should return to, again and again, not the hospital. Leave the hospital and his death here. I will take it from you. You do not need to feel guilty when you remember the good times. In our long lives, we have many, many relationships. Some are lasting, others too short. But that does not negate their wonder. You only had a few years with this boy, this wonderful child, but be blessed for the time you spent. Cherish those moments. Hold them in high regard. That is how you will push forward from your tragedy. That is how you can be full again, and let in love, and love yourself. I give this to you. I allow you this gift of letting go.*

When the ceremony ended many hours later, JD and Monica had purged their insides, vomiting and shit-ting out every last bit of toxins. O and the woman allowed them a moment alone. They lay in the hut by the crackling fire in each other's arms, a thin blanket draped over their bodies. They could barely move from exhaustion, but had never felt lighter. When O and the woman returned, O culled the smoke from the fire and blew it into the center of both of their foreheads. Then they went to sleep.

When they woke, they were no longer in the hut, seemingly far away. O and the woman had vanished. For a second, they wondered if it all had actually occurred or if they'd fallen into a crazy dream. They'd been enlightened, but O was not the shaman that would lead them to Gable to kill him. They found themselves getting up and leaving the jungle, heading to Guatemala City where they bordered a plane to Lima, Peru and then a smaller one to Iquitos. Neither expressed why they were going there—it felt like the only destination. O had given them many gifts and this would be the final one, a direct map to where their prey lay. When they got to Iquitos, a bustling city busier than any place they had been in some time, they were walking on a street searching for a ride into the Amazon and bumped into a woman. She had white hair but appeared to be younger than she looked, the lines on her face riddled with pain. A shaman hadn't taken the anguish away from her yet, but they could tell she desired it so. And then, they realized who she was. The familiarity in a face that had been splashed across newspapers years ago, the grieving mother whose daughter had been taken. Helene Stockton. Monica had met her early on during the case, and a recognition flashed across Helene's eyes too.

"What are you doing here?" Helene asked, practically trembling.

They hugged her because it seemed like the right thing to do.

"We were called here," they both said, because they began to speak as a unit sometimes, completely entwined.

"Me too."

"He is here," they said. "And we have come for him. To end him."

Helene nodded at this. "I've called a van to take me into the Amazon. I was waiting for it to show."

And as she said it, this van pulled up driven by a man in a big hat smoking a cigarette and leaning on the horn.

They all piled inside and took off out of the city, toward the pull of another jungle, a bigger one with more pockets for Gable to disappear. Each of them knew they were closer than ever to his demise, and it was only a matter of time.

# 19

ONCE AGAIN, THE IMAGES BEGIN TO FADE FROM THE top of the hut. The old woman lowers her hands after conjuring these visions, the flame burning low. Each time, William Clark arises from these journeys out-of-sorts. During them, he isn't bound to his addled body. Cannot feel the aches and pains, the inevitable creeping death. It is a moment of reprieve that she gives him, even though this is not her intention. She is here to torture him, and nothing could be more torturous than to forget one's traumas and then have them come rushing back.

The last image of his daughter Helene dissolves. She watches him, only her eyes remaining on the top of the hut before they vanish too. He lets out a cough that spills blood on the floor, wipes it away with the back of his hand.

"So, you are telling me that my daughter, along with my former employee and this ex-detective are on their way to ice me?"

The old woman flits her eyes to her bodyguard at

the door. "They are already here in the jungle. I have called each."

He lets out a bark of a laugh. "But you know me well?"

"I have studied you for some time, yes."

"So, you're aware that I am a slippery eel." He gives a wide grin. "I always manage to get myself out of difficult situations. Many times, foolish people have thought they had me, but never—"

"Foolish *people* maybe, but that is not me."

"Because you are not a person?"

"I am a person, yes, but I am also so much more."

"Why go through this whole...rigmarole? Why not just kill me now?"

"They deserve to witness your undoing. I have engineered this."

"My daughter...she may hate me; I am certain she does. But to kill me? She may change her mind once she's here."

"That is not what the universe tells me."

He looks up at the hole in the ceiling that views the star-ringed sky. "The universe... right."

"You still disbelieve me?"

"You sling a lot of out-there shit." He lets out a belch that seems full of darkness. As he exhales, it leaves his body in a cloud.

"That is what's in your system," she says.

"What causes me to do evil?"

"This the universe has not told me."

"So, you aren't as close with the stars as you think?"

"You can make jokes, if that's how you want to spend your final moments."

"How close is the party?"

She drags her body over to the hut's entrance, leans outside, and sniffs at the wind.

"An hour or two," she says. "They are walking."

"And how will I die? So, I can prepare and all."

She shakes a finger. "This I know but cannot say."

"Why?"

"Because you do not deserve a head's up."

"Because you are afraid that I will find my way free if you do?"

She does not answer. She eyes her bodyguard once more, and it's the first time he senses her fear. This woman has prided herself on being in control, but he is always in control. Even when his enemy believes he is not. It was how he managed fifty years in a business that ensnared some of the most important figures in history. They came to him for their secret desires and he bought their souls. For to cross paths with Gable once meant you were bound to him for life.

Out of the corner of his eye he sees the bodyguard remove a serrated knife from a sheath in the man's belt. The knife glints from the moonlight, telling William Clark that should he try anything his throat would be slit. But that would ruin their whole design. They needed him to remain alive to show his death to those he wronged. If he made a break for the entrance, there was nothing they could do. This would be his only shot. He has to try...

With all his might, he forces his weak legs to move. He picks up speed as he comes closer to the door. The old woman's mouth in a wide O. Her bodyguard with quick reflexes. The man pivots, the knife flipped to its blunt side as the handle is jammed into William Clark's temple. He drops to the ground, writhing. The bodyguard stands over him. Grabbing William Clark's shirt, he is pulled up to his feet and punched in the face. Blood drips down his nose, tastes like poison in his mouth.

"Do not do that again," the bodyguard says.

"Or what?"

"I will hurt you so bad. I will come close to killing you, show you the kind of pain you have never imagined, but you will still be hanging on by a thread. These next hours will be brutal."

"Do it."

The bodyguard takes the serrated edge of the knife and begins carving William Clark's face. His vision goes blurry, cast in a putrid red. He screams out until the old woman raises a hand and the bodyguard relents. William Clark staggers back, collapsing on the ground as his face throbs.

"Just fucking do it already, you cowards," he cries. "You lousy cowards. You can't do it, you can't."

"Stop!" the old woman thunders loud enough to shake his bones.

"Fine, what is next? You have more visions to show. Just fucking go ahead."

She culls her hands. "Others will be joining."

"Who? Who this time? Who else have I wronged?"

"Those with us no more. Your last evil deeds."

He knows precisely who she speaks of—The Doctor. An associate of his, a friend of sorts in a business that rarely allowed friendships. They met in the 70s in Miami, two flashy men in their separate Ferraris tearing down the streets. They controlled the drug trade together throughout each decade: in Miami, New York, Colombia, Europe, and lastly, Mexico. Javier was a relentless fuck just like him. A man with zero morals and a penchant for blow and the 80s band A-Ha. Whenever William Clark thought of The Doctor, he thought of the song "Take on Me." Its lyrics should be on the man's tombstone. A brilliant doctor himself before malpractice did him in, but an even more talented drug pusher. The Doctor could get whatever kind of candy one desired, have it shipped within the day. His arms extended across many continents. They made millions together, shared many a drink where they pontificated on the meaning of life. He did not intend to kill The Doctor. They escaped from Mexico on a boat and were to part ways as friends once they reached the shores of South America. But The Doctor came for him. And now he was to see this vision blasted across the top of the hut, as the old witch stokes the fire and throws her arms into the air to bring forth this recent tragedy.

Through his blood-stained eyes, The Doctor appears: thin as a whip, a white mustache dangling below his chin, wearing his signature purple John Lennon sunglasses.

The Doctor lets out a coke-filled smile as he beckons for William Clark to come join his murder.

## 20

HAVING FLED WITH THE DOCTOR FROM THE STATES
when the FBI realized his alias, it made sense for
William Clark to have him running their drug business.
He would handle the girls to the clients, The Doctor
would supply the candy. Both men in their late seven-
ties at the time, The Doctor had many years of contacts
who were as equally discreet. While he never knew of
The Doctor's exact origins, the man always alluded to
knowing Pablo Escobar, likely where he got in the biz.
The two met in Miami around '73 and once the Card
was up and running in the States in the mid 70s, The
Doctor would fly his plane over filled with bricks and
bricks of cocaine and then fly away. Likely back to Escobar, but William Clark never questioned. They re-
established their relationship in the late 2010s after
The Doctor was set up in the Pacific Northwest and his
operation became shut down after a bloodbath thanks
to one JD Storm. So, at the time both were looking to go
on the run. The Doctor swooped over, picked him up in

a van, and they wound their way down to Mexico before the feds had a chance to close in.

In a business where William Clark trusted few, The Doctor ranked as someone to at least be half-trusted. Both had enough shit on the other that evened them out. And The Doctor's drive was for more than simply money, a thrill-seeking spirit existed inside the man. It was part of the reason why The Doctor left his first occupation (although the malpractice suit didn't help—he did kill a woman on his operating table by accident). While medicine once gave him the god-like complex he sought, it wasn't sustainable enough. And it was hard to be high while operating (he learned that lesson after the dead woman). However, in the drug game one could be as tooted-up as one wished. It actually made for better relationships with clients, since they would want to know if his stuff was legit. What better way to prove it than to try it himself? So, this proved to be a lucrative venture for many, many years even after he and William Clark set up shop in Mexico.

The Doctor, no surprise, had his hands in many cartels' cookie jars. Why rely on one to buy in the goods when he could pit them against one another? Each of them had access to candy cane, but not the type of candy cane *he* could procure. While Escobar was long dead, connections born from that relationship still lasted. William Clark was making money with the girls and The Doctor was bringing in serious dough from the cane. The two had enough to stop and retire, something that they joked about.

"Maybe we should?" The Doctor said, puffing on a joint dipped in hash.

"And what would we do?"

"This?"

"This is not enough."

"What are you after then?" The Doctor asked, his eyebrows raised over his purple-tinted sunglasses.

"Never to be bored," William Clark said. "For boredom is death."

"A lot of other things can equal death," he said, referring to the many people who wanted their heads.

"At least with that we go out in style."

But then both reached an impasse. The cartels The Doctor sold to caught wind of one another and the different fees he charged. Meanwhile, the father of a girl William Clark kidnapped was a member of one of those cartels and sought revenge. Both these crucial situations meant the two had to leave pronto. While their safe house was being shot up, The Doctor pulled up in the same van he used to help them escape a few years back.

"Get in," The Doctor said. William Clark had a gun loaded, seemingly about to enter the house where bullets were already flying.

"I'm not running," William Clark said. "I'm tired of running."

The Doctor scratched his nose. "Are you tired of living?"

They heard a loud blast and a window shattered.

"Okay."

William Clark got inside and The Doctor floored it. They wound down back streets until they left town while William Clark watched the whole time from the back window for a chance they'd be followed. They drove until they reached a shore where a boat idled. A woman captained this boat, someone The Doctor vaguely referred to as a "friend." It did not matter to William Clark as they sailed away from Mexico. William Clark finally breathed once they couldn't see land anymore.

They celebrated that night. The Doctor brought a ton of candy cane (of course) and they tooted up as if they were young men again, racing their Ferraris along Miami Beach.

"We're untouchable," William Clark said.

"Cockroaches," The Doctor agreed.

"You are the only one, *the* only one in this world that I can rely on. My granddaughter, she's a rat, Brando and Astaire and the bodyguards all limp dicks. It's you and I, Doctor, till the very end."

The Doctor rubbed his bloody gums. "Fuck 'em."

"So, who's this "friend" of yours piloting the boat?"

"Eh, just a friend."

"Really?"

"Really. I mean, a long time ago our paths crossed amorously, but that boat has sailed, pardon my pun."

"Can she be trusted?"

The Doctor tipped down his John Lennon sunglasses on the beak of his nose. "Of course she can be trusted."

William Clark threw up his hands. "Whoa, whoa, Doctor. Only making sure."

"So, where are we headed?"

"Where do you wanna go?"

Since they left the shore, William Clark had a stirring in his belly. It began as a small seed tickling against his heart. But it had grown exponentially, telling him to head to Iquitos, Peru. He had never been to Iquitos before, not even Peru, so it was strange that he thought of such a specific place.

"Iquitos," he said, as if that was final.

The Doctor licked his bloody gums. "All right then, Iquitos it is."

The journey would take about two weeks, longer than anticipated but neither were really in a rush. There were enough provisions on board to eat sparingly. The captain was also adept at catching fish when she wasn't piloting. She didn't speak much and wore a heavy hat the entire time, which hid her face. When she spoke, it was usually in a mumble. But one night he found her underneath the stars by the stern. The Doctor had longed passed out after raging throughout the day.

"Mind if I join you?" William Clark asked. They had been on the water for about a week and his health ailments had started catching up. It couldn't have helped to do so much blow, but his lungs were definitely giving him trouble. For a long while he knew he was not long for this world. He didn't realize how soon his end could be.

"Your lungs," she said, as if she could read his mind.

"Yes," he coughed. "I haven't been diagnosed but likely cancer."

"It's always likely cancer," she mumbled.

It was the first time he saw her without a hat, since usually they were baked by the sun. Older than he imagined with clear eyes and a face that made it hard to remember when he looked away. As if she was a mirage of a woman rather than an actual one.

"I'm Kim," she said, holding out a hand. It was like butter when it slipped in his own.

"William Clark."

She shook her head, "That's not your real name."

"No. I used to go by Gable."

"That's not your real name either."

"No. Jay Howell."

He couldn't believe he was being so brazen. But he didn't care anymore. The pull to Iquitos was getting stronger and it seemed like nothing else mattered.

"Jay...Howell," she hissed, as if his name was a sin.

"So, you're a friend of The Doctor?"

She giggled. "Oh Javy? Yes, yes, a friend."

"You say that like..."

She beckoned with a finger. "Come here."

"Where?"

"Closer, you're so far away."

She was leaning against the edge, a siren on a rock. He stepped closer.

"When was the last time you were really kissed?" she asked, puckering her lips. "Really loved?"

He had to laugh. With his decaying body? No one attempted in so long. There were some girls he kidnapped who he tried out before he sold them, but they kissed like dead fish, no emotion behind it. He thought of his wife Vivienne, but their relationship had always been transactional. He provided her with a beautiful estate in tony Connecticut and she loved him back. There had been his operative Audrey Hepburn, who he kept hidden in a glass tower until she died. But that relationship had been one of lust, not love. The last woman he truly, truly loved had been Marilyn, one of his first operatives who wore a Marilyn Monroe mask. Marilyn had been scarred so bad when a mugger sliced her smile. She was looking for anyone to cling to. He gave her a purpose, a home at the Card. And she was one of the best. Until she took off in the night. He attempted to find her, but he'd been so hurt by her betrayal he was too afraid to face that rejection. No one else had ever made him feel that way. His beloved Marilyn. She had loved him once. He truly believed so. But then she also hated him with such passion. She wanted him dead. If she could've killed him, she would've. But it was easier for her to run away and never look back.

Now this Kim reminded him of her. Even in the woman's smile, which had similar scars at the ends, like it'd been sliced.

"You look..." he began.

A tooth slipped through that scarred smile, glinting from the moon. "Yes?"

"Like her. Your scars..."

He reached out to touch her scars, always bewitched by the pain that people had endured. He longed to know all about it, what brought them so much hurt. For he used hurt as his trade. To know one's secrets kept him powerful.

She stopped smiling quickly. "Oh, my scars."

"She had them too, this woman I...I really loved."

He found his eyes filling with water. This was a rare occurrence, and he'd forgotten what crying was like. Maybe the last time had been his childhood. And since then, he resolved not to let anyone make him weak.

She cocked her head to the side. "You really loved her? *Really*?"

Now it was his turn to be confused. "You speak like you know her."

Her laugh cut the air, and then she continued in a voice that mimicked Marilyn: "I am her."

He nearly fell to his knees. "*What?*"

"I mean, I've been her. We've all been her," she said, speaking like herself again. Although if he had to describe her voice, he couldn't. "Told we'd been loved and then hung out like laundry. Same story told time and again."

And trembling: "You sounded exactly like her. Like the voice she'd use when she was Marilyn."

"I thought she was Marilyn."

"I made her Marilyn. I created her."

"I think you've had too much candy cane."

"Listen," he thundered, getting in her face. "You *were* her, for a brief second. What the fuck was that? You tell me WHAT THAT WAS."

She met him nose-to-nose. "I'd push you away but you'd crumble to bits."

"You're a witch, we're being steered by a witch."

"I've seen this at sea before, the walls start to cave. We go a little *loco en la cabeza*, right? You, sir, need sleep."

"You tell me how you conjured her right then you sick twisted magician, or I will fillet you, that is a promise."

"With one breath I'd blow you over. You're practically in the grave."

He reached out to grab her when a shot went off puncturing the sky. The Doctor wobbling toward them with a pistol in hand.

"Get away from her," The Doctor cried, firing again and hitting the side of the boat.

"Are you fucking crazy?" William Clark yelled.

"You've been tooting all fuckin' day. Put that gun away."

"You touch her and you're eating this bullet."

He turned to Kim. "Tell him to chill the fuck out."

Kim gave a smug shrug. The Doctor fired again. William Clark's instinct kicked in; he'd been in enough close combats before. It was when he shined, despite his crumbling body. He lunged for The Doctor, knocking the man against the edge. The Doctor fueled up with candy cane strength; William throbbing with adrenaline. The gun went off again, causing Kim to yelp.

"You're mad," William Clark said. "Look at me. Look at me, Javier! She was Marilyn, do you hear me? She was fuckin' Marilyn and she's steering us to our doom. I'm not the one you want to ice."

"*You're* mad. We'd be dead if not for her. But I knew you would try something, you worm. You'd ice her and then you'd ice me."

The Doctor shot another bullet, the fourth if William Clark counted correctly. Meaning two remained.

"Why would I want to kill you?" William Clark asked.

"So there'd be no trail. That's the only way you'll survive. Ice everyone in your path. Because they'll find you if you don't. Too many want your head."

"And you're taking me to one of those fuckers who wants my head, aren't you? Aren't you, you son-of-a-bitch? You're getting paid, the both of you, to pass me off. That's why you saved me. Not out of any loyalty, is it?"

The Doctor didn't respond. Kim turned away.

"How much? How much are they paying you? I

need to know so I can understand how pathetic you are."

"Not being paid in money."

"Then what is it?"

The Doctor eyed Kim, and she gave the tiniest shake to her head. William Clark saw this all.

"But you need me alive, yes?"

The Doctor gave a firm nod. He waved the gun in the air.

"This has all been engineered."

"Since when?"

"Since, I...uh...got the call."

"From who?"

"I don't know who."

"Stop fucking with me."

"I don't."

William Clark turned to Kim.

"She don't either. So, this is how it's gonna work. We're gonna tie you up for the remainder of this trip—"

William Clark charged at The Doctor, causing the gun to fly. The Doctor too worried about falling off the boat, but William Clark grabbing the gun. He needed answers but he needed The Doctor iced more. He shot The Doctor clean between the eyes. He didn't have to look in those eyes long because The Doctor tumbled over the edge, plunging into the waters.

Kim's scream sounded like foghorns as he turned the gun on her.

"There's one bullet left. You drive this boat and let me off wherever you were taking me. You do this without giving me fucking sass and I will let you live at the end. Do you hear me?"

"Yes, yes I do."

"Good, now fucking get there fast."

For the next few days, he kept that gun on her. He didn't even let her sleep. To keep her awake, he peppered her with questions.

"Who hired you?"

"Javy."

"Who hired *him*?"

"I don't know. Truly. Javy needed a boat, I had a boat." She wiped away a tear. "I loved him, you know?"

"So did I."

"Do you always kill the ones you love?"

He thought back to the kill that had been the hardest, one of his earliest. Although he didn't actually kill Jake Barnum, who he hired around the inception of the Card. Jake had been like a son to him, but he became too much of a liability. So he had Marilyn ice him. Marilyn who'd fallen in love with Jake. He wouldn't let her fall in love with anyone.

"Because you love her the most," Kim said.

"Did I say all that out loud?" William Clark questioned, touching his lips as if they had betrayed.

"You didn't have to. So, why didn't you let this Jake live?"

"This was...almost fifty years ago. They were both gonna leave me, run off together. I couldn't lose them both."

"But you did."

"At least it was on my terms."

"Doesn't matter if they're both dead."

"She—I don't believe she's dead. At least not after she ran, maybe she is now, I don't know. They were gonna run away on a boat off the Hudson. He was waiting for her. She arrived with a gun and a bullet in his chest, like I told her to do. Because otherwise I would've iced her."

"What did she do after she killed him?"

"Beats me. Got on some other boat, disappeared. For a while, I tried to have her traced but came up empty. This was still a time when you really could disappear, not like now."

"What do you think is in Iquitos for you?"

"I don't—I don't know. My last chapter, I assume. Probably the end of the road for me."

"Who do you believe is waiting for you?"

She looked away from the ocean to gaze into his eyes.

"Probably someone who's been waiting a long time for this reunion."

"Yes, that would make sense."

He began coughing again, painting a handkerchief with blood.

"Because this will be your last reunion with anyone."

"Yes, likely."

"You've been a bad, bad man for a long, long time."

He took in the ocean, which held the remains of his once friend The Doctor. He missed him already.

"That's subjective."

"Always with a quick answer."

He made her a sandwich with bologna and Wonder Bread because that was the only provisions left. Three times a day. And a bucket for her waste while he'd turn away.

"You will honor our agreement?" she asked. "When we arrive? I have not protested. You will let me live?"

He held out the sandwich as she took a bite in the shape of a crescent moon.

"I will."

When they reached Iquitos days later, he could tell she was nervous. If he was being honest, he hadn't fully decided her fate. To let her live meant she could alert whoever engineered for him to arrive. But they likely knew anyway.

"I am sorry I had to kill Javier," he said. "It was never my intention."

He stared at her face. Again, when he'd look away, he couldn't remember her features.

"It always was," she said. "You just didn't know. Javy was never making it off the boat. He was a sacrifice."

"And you, what's your destiny?"

She brushed away the crumbs from her final sandwich from her mouth. "Only you know this. If you truly think you are not evil, you do not need to ice me too. I will let you off this boat and turn right back around. I will not exist to you anymore."

"That moment," he said. "When you sounded like her. You were her, right? She was speaking through you. My Marilyn?"

"If that's what you want to believe?"

"I know it in my gut. She's been speaking to me for some time."

"Then why piss her off even more?" She nodded at the gun in her face. "Also, you have one bullet left. You kill me and you're down to none. That's not great odds for what you're going up against."

"I've never allowed anyone the upper hand. You

understand this, don't you? If I let you live, fuck, it's taking too much of a chance."

"Everything is a chance."

"I'm sorry."

"Then you have already decided...?"

He fired the gun into her stomach, watched her clear eyes turn dark and then cloud over. She stumbled back, her guts spilling out, collapsing to the floor. He climbed off the boat into the swell of Iquitos: the honking cars, the dirt, smoke and chatter in the air. He was an old, old man who wasn't about to change. From an early age, he had revealed himself and nothing would cause him to sway. He had already forgotten her face, even her name. She was meaningless, her sole purpose in crossing his path to bring him here.

And now he would face his final test as he set his sights on the Amazon jungle.

## 21

THE WALK THROUGH THE JUNGLE FELT LIKE IT took eons for JD, Monica, and Helene. They didn't know where they were exactly going, only that a pull carried them all in the same direction. For JD and Monica, reaching Gable had been so long in the making, it was hard to imagine it was real. For Helene, it was even more complicated. Her father lay at the end of this journey, her father who she'd take part in killing.

What they didn't know was that traveling with them were two spirits whose lives had been altered from crossing paths with William Clark. The Doctor and Kim glided close behind, communicating to each other without words. They had been in love with each other thirty years ago, but time has no meaning once you're dead, so it was as if they'd never spent those years apart.

In the far distance, the light from a hut beamed like a flare in the midst of the darkness. It appeared as nothing more than a glowing dot, but they understood that was their destination. The calling within them ramping up with each closing step. Around them the sweet smell of humidity. Trees that created a path, ushered them along. Animals that hooted and growled but respectably kept their distance.

"Which one of us?" Helene asked, having a hard time swallowing. She took a gulp of water from a Nalgene bottle that had turned warm.

"Which one of us what?" Monica responded.

"Will be the one to end him?"

"Do you want that responsibility?" JD asked.

Helene hadn't thought this far. She didn't know if she wanted to live the rest of her life knowing she'd been the one to end his. It might be easier to only be a spectator.

"I say we all do it," Monica said. "Death by a thousand cuts. He deserves nothing else."

"Where will you go after?" Helene asked. She knew she'd return to Peter, good and kind Peter who worked for non-profits like she did and was the antithesis of the Stockton family she had married into. Would they stay in New York? Probably not. New York had eaten up too much of her soul, made her mean, held too many bad memories. They'd already been living in Peru for some time. And her son Brenton was never coming back, likely staying in Europe for the rest of his life. New York held no meaning to her anymore.

JD and Monica held hands, spoke in fits at the same time.

"We never..."

"Really discussed."

"I won't return to Florida," Monica said. "I'm no longer the woman who lived there."

"There's this place," JD began. "It's in Fiji. Matagi

Island. In my younger days when I had no possessions, I kept a postcard of it, tacked it up to my wall. Whenever things got dark, I'd lose myself in this idea of paradise. It was always what I was working toward... A volcano erupted and created the beach, so it's pure, mostly untouched."

Monica squeezed his hand. "So that is where we will go."

"I want to step into the waters and step out as someone new," he said. "Forget my past, and I believe I can, forget all this."

Monica rubbed his shoulder. "You will."

"We'll bury your son there, and we'll bury Annie," he said. "Keep them in our hearts but only our hearts, because the pain of their loss..."

"I know," Helene said. "I want that for Gracie too, so I can move forward."

"You can join us," Monica said.

"My boyfriend," Helene said, smiling because she had this wonderful man in her life again. "I'd have to see."

"There's a resort there we could get jobs at," JD said. "Live simply. Never return to the States, to real civilization."

"Yes, I would like that," Helene said.

"Gable," JD began. "Your father...he once promised all his operatives this type of paradise when we'd finally be able to retire. But it was a fool's fantasy. He would never let us go."

"I'm sorry for what he did to you."

"You are a victim of him too."

"It's hard to believe that I've come from him. That someone so..." She searched for the right word.

"Immoral...played such a significant part of my life. I have to worry if some of his influence seeped in?"

"It's what he was good at," JD said. "Making you think that his way was the right way, the only way. He was a magician like that."

"I have a memory," Helene said. "I'd gotten in a scuffle with a kid in my class, a nasty boy named Fred. He would pull the girls' hair. Well, I told my father this and after the playground one day when he came to pick me up, I saw him with Fred behind the alleyway. He was talking very close to Fred and Fred was trembling, like he'd seen... I don't know. The boy had wet himself, not even noticing the pee trickling down, and my father was relentless. Fred was crying, not loud sobs but quiet tears, so spooked. At the time I thought I'd never loved my father more for standing up to my bully, but Fred was never the same. He became withdrawn, heavy. Eventually he left school. The word was he went to psyche ward. A few years later he hung himself with his sheets. Just terrible. My friends and I weren't surprised, but I see it very differently now. Fred saw a glimpse of the devil, I truly, truly believe that. He let the devil in and never could get him out. I think that happened to my father, once. He must have been very little when it happened, but somehow, he was in the wrong place at the wrong time and the devil entered his soul. And he could never shake it. He had to live with this dual persona. And I'm not coming to his defense or anything, don't think that. He must pay for his sins. I'm just trying to understand what makes a man a man. And how he was never a man, he was more...or rather...less. All humans like him have been bitten. It's the only way to explain why they've done the horrible things they've done."

JD and Monica eyed each other. "We believe this too."

"And this shaman we seek, it will have the capabilities to overcome this beast. It has spent its life waiting for this very moment. That's what I feel deep inside of me. This hut that exists as a speck in the darkness is not a part of Earth. It's not a part of anything we can understand, but we have been invited, and this is our path. I am convinced my father will not make it to morning. This is the night when he will finally be snuffed."

The two spirits agreed with all that has been said. They floated beside this party, ready for the fireworks. For Kim who thought she might've been able to escape William Clark's snare and The Doctor who was flummoxed that his supposed best friend in the world could ever turn.

They would play a part in his demise just like the rest, even if they couldn't physically participate. Their spirits would be there to guide the others as the very plane they walk along becomes breeched and they enter another realm.

Then they can be at peace to pass along to where they belong, their energies freed from being stuck no longer.

## 22

As this final vision ends, it all starts to fall into place for William Clark. The old woman with the long, gray hair covering her eyes was not only someone he had known and wronged, but someone he had loved. It had been almost fifty years since he'd seen her last but there before him was Marilyn in the flesh.

"You know," she says.

"I think I always have."

A smile appears beneath the shadows. As he looks closer, he can see the scars he remembered and helped her hide with her mask. The slices at the end of her lips that made her smile even longer.

"I am no longer who you remember."

"Yes, I'm aware of that."

"When I left your orbit, I was a scared, little cat. You wanted me frightened, subservient. But that's not what I was born to be. I am fire."

As she said this, the bonfire between them grew even larger. He could see it reflected in the pools of her eyes.

"I almost left with him," she says, her voice changing from the old woman he first encountered to that of his beloved Marilyn. "Jake. He had his faults, but he was beautiful. He was beautiful to me, and that was enough. We could teach each other to be good again, because we once were until we were invaded. By you."

"Sweetie, you were a cunning temptress the second you shot out of your mother's cooch."

"Typical," she says. "Crude as always. That's the mask you wear."

"So, this is my final fate, to be analyzed by you?"

"Not analyzed, just held to the fire."

With that, a long flame broke away from the rest and caught on his shirt. He stamped it out quickly with his palm.

"There's more where that came from."

The bodyguard peers outside of the hut. In the distance, they hear footsteps approaching.

"Your reckoning," the bodyguard says.

"It speaks," William Clark jokes.

"You know who he is, right?" Marilyn says, as if she's ashamed. "Your son."

He stares at his supposed son, the likeness unmistakable to who he used to be. He'd known she was pregnant, but there were three men with the possibility of being the father. His operative Gregory Peck had raped her, Jake had loved her. Her relationship with him somewhere between the two in her eyes. His sperm would be the one to go the distance.

"It's a regular family reunion," he says.

"I do not think of you as my father," the bodyguard says.

"In the spiritual sense, definitely not," he says.

"I made it fine without you."

"Yes, living in the middle of nowhere doing your crazy mom's bidding."

His son stomps over and smacks William Clark across the face hard enough to knock him over. William Clark tastes blood on his lip.

"Yes, I deserve that."

"Do not let him get to you," Marilyn chides, and pets her son on the arm. William Clark can see the close bond they share, something he never had with his own children, Helene and Chip. "This is the moment you've been waiting for, that I've promised you all these years."

"So, I assume you're going to share with me your own origins from Marilyn to...whatever it is you are now."

"Marilyn is a ghost long gone, Norma too—my original name in case you forgot. They existed but are no longer a part of me."

"Then who are you?"

She shook her finger back and forth like a pendulum. "No, no, not yet. That will be at the end."

"Something to look forward to."

"You don't have much else."

"Tell me, what did I ever do that was so bad? You were a mess when you met me. Carved up and a shell of a woman. I covered your scars, gave you a purpose. You were my number one at the Card and had you not run, I would've ruled it with you till the end. We could've died old together." He glanced over at his son. "With him too."

She blew a raspberry. "You would've helped raised him?"

"If I knew he was really mine, yes. I was constricted by my family, Vi and the kids. We were never meant to be, but you and I..."

"You're lying."

"Aren't you heightened enough now to know if I am? Your powers?"

"It doesn't work like that."

"I'm not lying, baby." He steps closer and she hangs back. "May I...?" he asks, reaching out to part her hair.

His son jumps between them, protecting his mother. "I can't let you..."

"I just want to...really see your face. Promise. No funny stuff."

Marilyn gives her son a precise nod and he steps aside, resuming his place at the entrance. The footsteps even closer now. William Clark can't quite see who's following him yet from outside the hut, the darkness swallowing too much. But he doesn't care about that now. He wants to see what she's become.

She acquiesces and he parts her long, gray hair, tucks it behind her ears. Staring back at him is a face similar to the woman Kim who he killed. He could stare forever but not remember it completely. It's the face made up of a thousand others, all those he burned uniting together for retribution. He's cast into her clear eyes where he dips into the pool of her origins. Like he's attached by a bungee cord, he's yanked inside of her, filling her body whole, rocking around in her brain. It's a murky place he glides around, searching for what made her. He locates a gold pebble he squeezes in his fist, and it beams her story across the black sky. She's just shot her lover Jake Barnum, who collapses in defeat. Blowing him a final kiss, she takes off through the boat terminal until she's plunged into the reality she now faces: one without the dream escape with the one she truly loves, forced to return to the one she despises.

"Fuck that," she said out loud, and then thundering at the heavens: "Fuck. That."

# 23

Before she shot him, Marilyn told Jake Barnum her real name: Norma. Much like the real Marilyn Monroe, she always felt like two people housed in one body. Norma, who strived to be good but had a tough upbringing. A father who left when she was a baby. A mother who never should've been a mother. They lived in a trailer park in Ohio, her mother often gone. From an early age, she was left alone to her own imagination. As a teen, she worked at a local Drive-Thru, one of the first in her town. She'd save up all her money to go to the movies, fascinated with their other worlds where stars shone bright. Marilyn Monroe's films were her favorite. She'd get a big soda and be transported by *Gentlemen Prefer Blondes* and *Some Like It Hot*. Marilyn Monroe was a girl who rose from her own tough beginnings. It made her convinced she could do the same.

New York had always been on her radar. Her mother went through a cycle of terrible boyfriends, the last one getting handsy over the breakfast table, so

Norma clocked him with the toaster that was still plugged in. A thin line of blood streaked from his temple. He slumped over while her mother screamed. She had a suitcase already packed, bought a bus ticket, and was gone. Arriving in New York City with a few bucks to her name, she started waitressing at a diner near Times Square. She roomed with three other girls in a studio apartment, but had never been more alive. That was until she got mugged and her smile slashed. The streets became evil, she became a shut-in, and then she met Gable.

She'd lost her waitressing job but got another one as a cigarette girl at a fancy club. The job was nights, the lights dim and with enough concealer, she could cover up her mutilated smile. She also wore her blonde hair down to help. Someone would have to part her hair and look really close in the darkness to locate the abuse.

Gable was a big roller, like most guys who patronized the joint. He smoked fat cigars, he tipped well. The club had dancing acts; girls who usually went topless but never more. She didn't mind.

"Pall Mall?" she asked him. He was dressed in a suit like a penguin with a top hat that went out of style twenty years earlier.

"Only cigars for me I'm afraid."

"I've never smoked one."

"Well, you haven't lived then."

He touched her hand and she felt a shiver rocking her bones. She needed to get to know this man, believed it in her heart.

"I'm off at two," she said. "Usually have a smoke out back, but I could try a cigar."

At two, she hurried out and didn't see him. Figuring

he likely forgot, she was about to head home when a match lit down the alleyway and he stood there with two cigars in hand.

"*Pour vous.*"

"Thank you."

She coughed up a storm the first few sucks but then got the hang. He nodded in approval. He had a face that belonged to a president. The kind of guy who took up space in the room.

"So, what's a lovely girl like you working in a dump like this?"

"Oh, I don't think it's a dump."

"Hey, you'll light your hair on fire if you don't move it out of the way."

He went to part her hair, saw what she was hiding. The knife-marks that traced from the ends of her smile all the way to her cheekbones. She dropped the cigar in a puddle.

"Oh."

"That's all right," he said. "I'm sorry."

"Sorry for what?"

"For whatever someone did to you. I'd take out his heart if I could, stomp it to bits."

"How'd you know it was a guy?"

"It's always a guy, I'm afraid."

"It was a mugging. It's in the past."

"But it still affects you."

"Well, sure."

"I might have a solution."

They went back to his office on Park Avenue. She'd never been to Park Avenue before. He had a receptionist in the front who he introduced as Bette. Her face looked familiar, but she couldn't place where from.

Bette barely acknowledged them, pounding away at her typewriter. They went into his office that had a view which made her gasp.

"Oh my."

"Beauty, huh? Straight shot down Park Avenue. Looks even better during the day."

She took in the room. A mahogany desk, nice wet bar, a golden pig as art. "What kind of business do you do?"

"I'm in the business of desires."

She let out a sigh. "Oh, one of those. Nice digs for a pimp."

"No, no, you misunderstood, I'm not a pimp. I have very wealthy clients who come to me when they are looking for the obscure."

She scrunched her face in confusion.

"I'm a collector of sorts and people come to me for rare things."

"Oh, I get ya."

"Like those cigars we smoked, well that you took a puff of."

"Sorry."

"No, no, just that they were rare, special. I trade in specialties. What someone desires but never thought they could ever have. For the right price, I can get it. It's called the Desire Card."

"The Desire Card," she said, feeling the words in her mouth.

"I'm looking for a new trainee actually. Are you bound to being a cigarette girl forever?"

She laughed. "I don't think that's anyone's lifetime dream."

"Did you recognize Bette at all?"

"The receptionist? Sorta. Her face was familiar."

"Ever seen *All About Eve*?"

"Well, sure, I've seen all the old movies. My favorite is Marilyn Monroe."

"Is it?" He held up a finger, went to his closet, and pulled out a mask. "Try it on."

"What is it?"

"Marilyn Monroe herself."

The mask fit snug over her face, like it had always meant to be a part of her. Looking in the mirror, she was a dead ringer for Marilyn Monroe. Not a mask that looked like something a kid would wear on Halloween, it was as if young Marilyn Monroe had been resurrected.

"Wow."

"Right?"

"Why the masks?"

He made them two glasses of bourbon, passed one over to her. "I'm a collector. Of valuable things, sure, but also of souls. Souls that need uplifting. You've been hurt in life. You've experienced much pain, but that doesn't have to be your story. It could be a chapter that has closed. With the mask, you are no longer your past. You are here, now."

She admired herself in the mirror, admitting that she was more confident than she'd been in a while.

"So, what would I do for you?"

"As a trainee, help me facilitate these wishes."

These wishes started off benign: hard-to-get cigars, art, diamonds. She was falling in love with Gable as well. He took her to fancy restaurants, bought her a mink, moved her out of the studio apartment with three other roommates. Looking back, she realized she was being groomed, but she'd never been happier.

The first kill was a man on the Upper East Side, billed to her as a guy who abused his wife. He'd hit her just too many times and she wanted him removed. The cops did nothing and she was tired of using make-up to conceal her black eyes. Marilyn would go to his hotel room. He'd think she was a call girl. When they'd have a drink, his would have a poison pill. She'd leave before he had the chance to even touch her.

Afterwards she cried in the rain. She'd obviously never taken a life before. Gable was there to calm her down, telling her she made the world a better place. That was how it was at first. The kills all being justified until they blurred and he no longer tried to give her reasons. The new reason was the amount a client paid. That was all that mattered.

She did his bidding for years until Jake Barnum came along. She told herself she was in love with Gable, but had lost all feelings toward him. Jake was kind in a way she'd never experienced before. She had dreams of running away with him but knew that Gable would never let her go. She was his toy and would never be anything more. And when she pulled the trigger and killed Jake, she even thought about turning the gun on herself.

Running down the streets with a gun stuffed in her bra, she had no idea where she would go. Over the years she saved up some money. Mostly tips from clients, since Gable handled the financial transactions. She'd taken a bus from Ohio when she was barely eighteen. She fled before and she'd do it again. So she bought a ticket for a bus down to Florida. Waited at Port

Authority with a knot in her stomach. Glancing back and forth, everyone could be a member of the Card, ready to ice her. Even on the bus, she stayed awake for the entire journey. Ready to grab the gun and plug a son-of-a-bitch if need be. Gable would realize when she didn't return right away that she had left. He'd go to her apartment and wait for her. He'd likely monitor the airports, the train stations with operatives, likely Port Authority too. But somehow, she got lucky. The big man in the sky was looking out for her for once.

In Tampa, she jumped off the bus into a blast of heat. Being far away from New York City was the goal, and Florida wasn't far enough. There was a boat that went to the Yucatan and she got on board. Mexico didn't feel safe either, since Gable had connections there and she stood out, so she got on another boat that took her to Guatemala. She once read a book about the jungles of Central and South America and heard of a place called El Péten. She could go into the jungle and be safe, at least from him. So, she bought a backpack and descended into its heart. She lived off leaves for a while until she was approached by a native man and woman. Neither of them spoke, but deep down she knew she had to follow them. They had a tiny hut where they were taking part in a ceremony. With their eyes, they told her to join. She drank what she later learned was *ayahuasca* and her world opened up. Over the course of the next six hours, she found demons that were representations of Gable and defeated them each time. At the end of her journey, she awoke outside of the hut, laying in the dirt. The man and the woman standing over her.

*I am O*, he said, with his eyes. *And who you were*

*does not exist anymore. You are born here and you are meant to be a shaman. That is your calling. All of your past lives have trained you for this. And it is an important task. You have come across an evil being in your past lives. This being has circled around you for some time, but you have always managed to evade its snare. I will train you. It may take years for you to be at a level to take on this being. Time is not important. You will fight when you are ready and it will be on your turf, this world. You are pregnant?*

*Yes, it is his baby*, she replied with her own eyes.

*He will be trained too.*

*He?*

*Yes, you are carrying a boy. A boy that will be on the precipice between good and evil. We will make sure he stays on the right side. When the time is right, I will let you go. You will call this presence to you and you will light it on fire. That is the only way to defeat such a force.*

So, she stayed in El Péten for most of her adult life raising a son she named Fuerte, meaning "strong." He was a beautiful, healthy boy and under the teachings of O became a gentle man, except if anyone messed with his mother. Years later, after she ascended to becoming a great shaman, her powers at their peak, fully intermingling with this world and beyond, O told her it was time to go. His area in El Péten was for training and she must face this dark entity on her own. She wept at the loss of this father figure, the only one in her life who had ever been truly kind. She hugged him and the woman by his side, who never revealed her name. And she set off with Fuerte. She was an older woman by then, but stronger than ever. O told her to go where her heart called to settle. They took a boat down to Iquitos because for years it had been the place she dreamed. From there, they punched into the Amazon and wandered for days, weeks, maybe even months until they discovered a hut in the middle of nowhere. By then, they could fully live off the land without a problem; a jungle had been her home for forty plus years. Once they settled in the hut, she sent out to call to this dark entity she once called Gable. For a long time, she waited until there was a contact, culling the flames to the sky in search for him. Finally, she felt a connection. His heart weakened, likely from age and sickness, but she heard its beating. He was closer than ever, meaning he had left the States. He was fleeing to her neck of the woods, on her turf like O had promised. Now it was time to bring everyone else he wronged to assist in his demise. It wouldn't be easy. There was no guarantee she'd be victorious. But her life was ending and it was time to face this battle.

*You are ready*, she heard O say across the wind, as she blew into the fire and saw Gable's gnarled image, heading her way.

## 24

"I've arrived," William Clark says. "And I've had my Ebenezer Scrooge moment. Now it's time to pay the piper I presume?"

Marilyn (and he refused to think of her in any other way) sneered. He could tell she enjoyed torturing him in this way. Her whole adult life since she left had led to this and her face seemed melancholy.

"You've spoken of me as a dark entity, compared me to the devil, said I've been possessed." He looks at his aged hands covered in purple veins and wrinkles, as if they could give a clue. "But I am just a man. Don't you see? Or do you not want to? You've convinced yourself I am much more, but this is me...flesh and blood."

She blows at the fire. "I'm aware you will try and talk your way out of this because you have before. Not anymore."

The footsteps they've heard draw closer. The party has arrived. They peer through the opening of the hut, wary. Fuerte ushers them inside. JD, Monica, and his daughter Helene, barely recognizable with her ghost-white hair. And the two spirits he recently murdered hovering by the entrance.

"Please, come in," Marilyn waves. A smile on her face like he's never seen. She's practically giddy.

JD growls while Monica gives him a steely glare. Helene, the most emotional of the three, fighting everything in her not to cry.

"Helene," he says, holding his hands out as if imploring her forgiveness. She looks away.

"I have called you here for one reason and one reason only," Marilyn says. She reaches into a pouch hanging from her waist and pulls out three rusted daggers, which she hands out.

"I will give you all the honor of drawing his first blood," Marilyn continues, her eyes on the fire. "You will destroy his human form and I will take care of the rest. That is how it must be done."

"I am riddled with disease," he says. "I am already dead, don't you understand? You don't need to be murderers."

"It's too late for that," JD says. He can spy the old James Dean in the man: cunning and ruthless, why he'd been hired. James Dean was one of his best operatives across all the decades he ran the Card. Former soldiers were always shaken up enough by their pasts to lose all their moral impulses for him. He never expected James Dean would turn. Assumed he could even take the Card over from him when he passed.

JD holds up the dagger, ready to strike. "I've been waiting a long time for this. Tell me. Tell me one thing."

William Clark raises his eyebrows, gesturing for JD to continue.

"Annie," he says, and William Clark has to think for

a second who that is. He's met many people in this long life and she was there for only a moment. JD's ex-girl-friend, the one he went to hide with when he fled.

William Clark lets out a smile, showing his rotting teeth. There'd been no toothpaste on the boat over and it had been likely a month since he gave them a good brushing. "You want to know if I turned her, right? But do you really want to know?"

JD clutches the knife. "I do."

"She did. For even less than you'd think. A couple thousand bucks if I remember correctly."

JD charges at him, the dagger held high. He plunges it into William Clark's collarbone. William Clark lets out a howl, collapsing to his knees. JD pulls out the dagger, spraying blood across the hut. With quivering hands, William Clark tries to staunch the flow of blood.

JD is heaving, a beast awaiting a final kill. But Marilyn holds up a hand, preventing him from continuing. He's off in another world anyway, likely thinking about Annie who he tried to believe hadn't given him up to the Card years ago. That she was innocent. But no one who comes in contact with the Card can ever be innocent again.

"Next," Marilyn coos, directing her energy toward Monica. And while she wasn't directly affected by William Clark, the pent-up anger from losing her son, from being unable to bring Gracie back home when she was a detective, causes her to leap at William Clark, stabbing him in the side. Blood paints her face as she pulls out the dagger. He lets out a cry that echoes up to the sky. She finds solace in JD, as they hug, a weight leaving their bodies. They can begin anew now that he will be gone. It is only a matter of minutes.

Marilyn nods at Helene. "Daughter," she says. "Be the one to end it for good."

Helene hesitates at first, her knees knocking. She could tell herself over and over that this is what must occur, but there is a difference between reality and dreams. She's envisioned ending her father many times along this journey, but now as he kneels before her bleeding out from two open wounds, she doesn't know if she has the power to deliver the final blow.

"Do not be scared," Marilyn thunders. "He is not your father. A monster writhes before you now, one that will continue its slaughter. You are strong. I have called you from far away because you are the one to end—"

"This witch's babble," William Clark cries. "Do not listen, Helene. Of everyone in my life, I cared about you the most."

"Don't listen to him," Marilyn warns.

"Stop!" Helene shouts, blocking her ears. She cannot hear anymore. The push and pull of emotions too great to bear. She hates him with every fiber, but a trace of love still exists. He was never directly cruel to her; he saved that for everyone else, including Gracie.

"You killed her," she says, the dagger raised. "My baby."

"Technically, I—"

"Stop making excuses. You didn't need to take her. You don't know what that did to me."

"Helene," he says. "I had no choice. They were coming for me. I needed—"

She doesn't let him speak anymore, plunging the dagger into his chest. He's surprised at first, probably thinking he could convince her otherwise, but she no longer lives inside of her body. She's a being of pure rage that stabs him again and again: his gut, his throat, the dagger right in his eye. He allows this to happen, unable to fight back. She stabs him until he's unrecognizable, his blood painting her face in a mask. She is the demon now and has to be wrangled by Marilyn before she hurts herself. Marilyn gets the dagger from her, looks deep into Helene's eyes.

"You can return from this," she tells her. "You have done what is needed. Let me do the rest."

She motions for JD and Monica to take care of her. Helene falls into their arms as they attempt to soothe. Now it is her turn to finish the job. The spirits of The Doctor and Kim watch over her, guiding her over to his mutilated body. She takes his face in her hands, her wrinkled lips moving in for a kiss. She kissed this man many times years ago, but this would be their final one. His lips are bloody and sliced, but she begins to suck. She turns herself into a vacuum, sucking whatever has existed inside of him. His dead belly rumbles, whatever she has unearthed not pleased with being removed. But she draws upon all she has been taught from O, her lifetime of shamanic influences until they all can visualize a snake-like entity squirming from his stomach up to his chest, slithering through his throat, until she catches it in her own mouth like a burning ball of lava. She flings back from him as Fuerte intervenes, dipping a torch into the flames and lighting the cadaver of William Clark on fire. The body still moves as the flames chew it to ash. She tells her son goodbye with her eyes and he nods in acceptance because they both knew this was always how it would end.

She flies past them all out of the hut, clamping her jaw shut out of fear that she will release this demon back into the world. She can hear the rest of them running out of the hut after her. Looking over her shoulder, the hut is consumed with flames as it collapses. She sets her sights on a pool of black water glinting in the moonlight.

"NOW!" she tells Fuerte with her mind as he throws the flaming torch at her and it catches in her hair. She erupts, the fire eating her clothes as she winds her way toward the water. She can feel the demon writhing in her mouth, screaming its banshee yell to try to escape. It breaks her teeth, rips her tongue, bites at her throat, but she clamps her fiery hands over her mouth and plunges into the black waters. The fire seeps through her nose, the smoke choking the demon and her. It has been a long road that has led to now and she can see Fuerte and the rest of them above the water watching her thrash around. She is the strongest being in existence as the flames crackle her body to ash. The demon grows weaker, her last sensation being whatever it considers its heart exploding. And then there is stillness. She's at the bottom of these waters, crossed-legged and awaiting death, which arrives as a sweet embrace. Her eyes close and there is nothing, only peace, as she ascends and whatever possessed William Clark descends, neither existing in the living world anymore.

## 25

On Matagi Island, a volcano erupted many millennia ago coating the beach with black sand. This is where JD and Monica sit as they watch the waves lick the shore. She rests her head on his shoulder, and they breathe in the ocean together. A beautiful resort behind them where they work in security. Helene and Peter have also moved to the island where they started a non-profit with the island's owners bringing literacy campaigns across the Fijian islands. The two married on this beach and her son and grandbaby attended. Monica was a maid-of-honor and JD Peter's best man. They have never spoken of the events that occurred in the Amazon, nor ever will, for to mention the devil gives it power.

After work each day, they come to the beach and slip their toes into the black sand. They watch the sunset, then usually have a meal at the local shack that serves conch. The days and night bleed into one another, but not for long, because Monica is expecting JD's child. It will be a baby girl and they decided to name her Marilyn. Monica is nine months pregnant, and her feet are swollen. But they walk down to the beach together still because that is their ritual.

Nothing on this Earth fills them with more desire.

This night, as the sun gives its final dip, her water breaks.

## ACKNOWLEDGMENTS

Thank you to everyone who helped bring The Desire Card Series to publication. My agent Sam Hiyate and his staff at The Rights Factory. The series editor James Reasoner and everyone at Wolfpack Publishing and Rough Edges Press: Patience Bramlett and Mike Bray. Ben Tanzer and Lori Hettler for publicity. Also, to my Dad who loved old movies and would've gotten a kick out of the movie star masks. Thank you all.

# ABOUT THE AUTHOR

**Lee Matthew Goldberg** is the author of eight novels including *The Ancestor* and *The Mentor* and the YA series *Runaway Train*. His books are in various stages of development for film and TV off of his original scripts. He has been published in multiple languages and nominated for the Prix du Polar. *Stalker Stalked* will be out in Fall '21. After graduating with an MFA from the New School, his writing has also appeared as a contributor in *Pipeline Artists*, *LitHub*, *The Los Angeles Review of Books*, *The Millions*, Vol. 1 *Brooklyn*, *LitReactor*, *The Big Idea*, *Monkeybicycle*, *Fiction Writers Review*, *Cagibi*, *Necessary Fiction*, *Hypertext*, *If My Book*, *Past Ten*, the anthology *Dirty Boulevard*, *The Montreal Review*, *The Adirondack Review*, *The New Plains Review*, *Maudlin House*, *Underwood Press*, and others. His pilots and screenplays have been finalists in *Script Pipeline*, *Book Pipeline*, *Stage 32*, *We Screenplay*, the *New York Screenplay*, *Screencraft*, and the *Hollywood Screenplay* contests. He is the co-curator of *The Guerrilla Lit Reading Series* and lives in New York City. Follow him at LeeMatthewGoldberg.com.

9 781685 491529